A Frost in
the Night

EDITH BAER

A Frost in the Night

SCHOCKEN BOOK NEW YORK

Library of Congress Cataloging-in-Publication Data

Baer, Edith.
A frost in the night.
Summary: Relates the experiences of a young
Jewish girl growing up in a city in southern Germany
during the period of Hitler's rise to power.
[1. Jews—Germany—Fiction. 2. Germany—History—
1918–1933—Fiction] 1. Title.
[PZ7.B1388Fr 1988]   [Fic]   87-42994
ISBN 0-8052-0857-7

For my parents
Julius and Martha Baer

1887–1942   1901–1944

IN REMEMBRANCE

There fell a frost in a night of Spring
It fell on the tender young flowers blue,
They withered away and wilted . . .

HEINRICH HEINE
after a folksong heard on the Rhine

A Frost in the Night is a work of fiction, distilled from memory, love, loss and sorrow. Thalstadt, though it resembles my native city in many ways, could have been any German city in the early thirties, and the events seen here through the prism of fiction might have happened in any of them. . . .

E.B.

PART ✦ ONE

"What Better Place ...?"

1 ❦❦❦

For as long as she could remember, there had always been
Thalstadt, and she in it. There were winters and there were
springs; and on spring mornings, before the city awoke, the
scent of the white chestnut blossoms drifted from the plaza
and filled the air. In any season it seemed a place suffused
with light, a time for growing, for unfolding. If there were
shadows, she was unaware of them, or at most they seemed
transient things, with no more substance and menace than
the shadows the sun threw against the rugged wall of
Grandfather's house.

Grandfather's house—Eva always thought of it as that,
though they all lived in it: Eva and her parents and
Grandfather in the apartment where her father had grown
up; her cousins, Ella and Uschi, with Uncle Ludwig and
Aunt Gustl upstairs. But it was Grandfather who had built
the house and had lived in it longest; and like Grandfather,
it possessed an unadorned solidity and stubborn changelessness. Eva could not imagine a time when Grandfather's
house would no longer stand, any more than she could
imagine a day when Grandfather would no longer be with
them.

He was a small man, tidily put together, with smooth

brows over cool old eyes, and a short white beard that came to a neatly trimmed point. A tiny golden bear, symbol of his maternal family name, dangled from his watch chain over his gently rounded vest. He rose early each morning, and often Eva and he would breakfast quietly together at the round dining-room table. With a deft flick of his wrist he would shave off the tip of his egg and hand it to her, and she would solemnly scoop out the little white dab with her spoon and savor its blandness for a moment on her tongue before she took the first sip of her hot cocoa. She never paused to wonder about this morning ritual so ceremoniously performed by them. Only later, as she grew older and heard stories about Grandfather's youth in a poor village family, where eggs and butter and even milk had been a rare treat, she thought about it and felt she understood. And in some other room, distant in time and place, she would see a small boy, the youngest of many children, receiving a coveted gift—a taste of the lone morning egg reserved for his father . . . .

Over his coffee, Grandfather would tease Eva with questions about arithmetic and other tricky things. "What's heavier—a pound of feathers or a pound of lead?"

"They're—both the same!" It didn't make sense, but the perfectly sensible answer she had given the first time he had asked had turned out to be the wrong one, to Grandfather's lasting amusement.

"We'll make an Einstein of you yet," Grandfather said in his soft Rhenish drawl. Though he had come to their South German city in the province of Swabia as a young man many years before, his speech had never lost the gentle cadence of his native Rhineland. But it was a deceptive gentleness: Grandfather was a dry and sober man who permitted himself no outward show of emotion. Eva had heard it said that he was not an easy man to deal with; his tongue was tart and his studied aloofness intimidated some and drew suppressed smiles from others. But Eva, neither awed nor amused, would think of the bland egg under its smooth, brittle shell and feel that she knew his secret.

She knew his house, too, from top to bottom, the way she knew her favorite books from cover to cover. At night, by lying very still and with her eyes shut tight in the dark, it was even possible to see the house by ear. The way the stairs creaked beyond the wall, for instance, made her see the people who walked on them. When the Haeberles' lodger slowly climbed up the stairs, the sounds his shoes made said very plainly: *holprecht, holprecht, holprecht.* This was remarkable, for the Haeberles' lodger's name happened to be Herr Holprecht.

The Haeberles lived one floor up, across the hall from her cousins Uschi and Ella. The pipe-smoking old man in his knitted gray vest had "worked for the city" all his life; his large wife and their aging daughter, Gertrud, went about their chores in felt slippers and shapeless housedresses pulled over their sagging breasts. The women's booming voices and blustering cordiality put Eva vaguely on guard. She did not tell her cousins, who seemed unaware of anything disquieting beneath the musty kitchen odors and stale tobacco smoke that clung to the hastily tidied rooms. Ella, in particular, was a frequent and noisily received visitor next door. She even was allowed to bring steaming soup bones to Gertrud's huge German shepherd, Wotan, who once had snarled at Eva on the street when she had tried to pet him.

"If you tell your grandfather, Eva Bentheim, I'll tell your

cousins not to play with you," Gertrud had snapped, ruffling Wotan's fur to soothe his feelings.

Having no sisters of her own to play with, Eva told no one. But ever since, when she ran out of excuses and reluctantly accompanied Ella on one of her visits across the hall, she held on to her cousin's hand in front of the Haeberles' door. Inside, she quickly pulled past the kitchen where Wotan lay drowsily on his rumpled blanket, lifting a rheumy old eye and snorting his curt, inscrutable growl.

Sometimes Gertrud told stories about the time before the war when she had been a pupil at Thalstadt Girls' School, and the queen, who had endowed the school, had come with her entourage for an inspection visit.

"I'll never forget it as long as I live," she would say, and blow the froth off her afternoon beer. "The queen with her big white hat and parasol, and her officers in their smart white uniforms saluting us girls in our fancy dresses and flower wreaths. . . ."

She pushed a lank strand of graying hair behind her ear and slapped Ella's back with a thud. "*Ja*, girlie, those were the days, before the Republic, when we still had our king and queen. . . ."

The other tenants were less pervasive presences in Grandfather's house. Keeping to themselves across the hall from Eva's family were two elderly sisters, both widows "of professional men," as they would tell Eva's mother on the landing in hushed and faintly condescending tones. Still more remote were the top-floor occupants—Herr Chief Engineer Hartmann and his wife and two grown sons, and Herr City Archivist Demuth and his round, flustered Frau—who turned up only in passing now and then in the stairwell.

Way up at the top of the last creaking steps was the attic with its clean smell of starlight and dry wood, where Eva's mother and Anna, the Bentheims' cook, kept wax-sealed jars of pickles and preserves. Under the eaves, Eva and Uschi rummaged among dusty trunks, three-legged pieces of furniture, and an ancient hatstand still holding aloft their long-dead grandmother's plumed hat.

Standing on tiptoes at the high attic windows one could see much of Thalstadt and know the rest by heart: the church spires and modern buildings towering over the narrow gabled houses of the Old City; the Rathaus, the Town Hall on the nearby Marktplatz; the Old and New Castle facing the Schlossplatz, the Castle Plaza with its flower beds and chestnut trees and the Angel of Peace atop the Marble Column. And all around the city were the green, sloping hills called The Heights, dotted with fenced-in houses in their gardens.

Eva's school was somewhere behind the trees on one of these hills, and so were the houses of some of her classmates. From time to time she would hear her mother say how nice it would be to live in a small house of their own on The Heights, and Aunt Gustl, who did not often agree with her sister-in-law, would pause in her knitting and remark that, as far as *her* family was concerned, she had often told Ludwig the same.

But Grandfather had made it clear that he would never agree to move from his house, and his sons would not leave him behind. The situation suited Eva perfectly. She liked living in the bustling center of Thalstadt, in a big house with a cellar and an attic of which she knew every cobwebbed corner. She liked having Ella and Uschi as close by, almost, as if they were her own sisters.

And one of the things she liked best about Grandfather's house was the family store.

The store, facing Wieland Square under the sign J. BENTHEIM & SONS, had been founded by Grandfather, who had "guided it toward modest success from humble beginnings," as he was fond of saying in his mock-serious, ironic voice. On the ground floor was the stationery department with its neat stacks of notebooks and reams of white paper; its glass-enclosed fountain pens and marble inkwells, paperweights, and blotters; its gleaming rows of leather school satchels and briefcases; and the thick rolls of sturdy brown wrapping paper that Viktor, the salesman, tore off against the razor-sharp edge with such aplomb. Each spring and fall, Eva and her cousins would get their school supplies for the new semester in Grandfather's store. Actually, it was now mainly Uncle Ludwig, Grandfather's elder son, who carried on the stationery business, with Grandfather stopping by for daily extended visits to keep an eye on the proceedings and magnanimously hand out unsought advice. The realm of Eva's father was the bookstore on the second floor.

In all of Thalstadt this was perhaps Eva's favorite place: a place to browse, to read, to help her father sort and shelve his books, to spend hours in on vacation and after school. Customers climbed up the steps from the ground floor, took their time looking over the books, and left—sometimes with purchases, more often without. It was "the times," her father said; many people were out of work and had no money to buy books. Still, enough did come to keep her father busy answering inquiries, advising shoppers in his reserved yet animated way, and retreating to his small office to order additional books—perhaps the latest novel by Thomas Mann or his brother Heinrich, or by the American writer, Upton Sinclair.

Meanwhile, squatting on the floor beside the low shelves of the children's section, Eva had selected a book of her own and soon was immersed in the world between its covers. Through the windows looking out on the new steel-and-concrete structure of Hallenbeck's department store across the street, the afternoon sun streamed in, casting flickering lights on the pages.

Starting a new book was very much like meeting people for the first time, and if one liked them, coming back to be with them again and again. The more different the people and their families were from one's own, the more fascinating they were to be with. In one such family, the kindly Herr and Frau Professor Müller not only had five children of their own but readily took in three more, whose parents—traveling circus performers—had met an untimely death on the high wire while passing through the Müllers' town. The book was titled *A Happy Family*, and Eva, comparing her serene and solitary life to the high drama and excitement in the large Müller household, considered the title entirely appropriate.

When at last her father's amused voice recalled her into time and reality, the store lights had come on and were ready to be switched off again for the night. With the book tucked under her arm to "finish the chapter," she groggily watched her father lock up the store and followed him up the stairs to their apartment on the next floor.

2 ⚱⚱⚱

For a while, when Eva had been very young, Detta had stayed with them, too. Now Eva remembered little more than the angle of the nanny's hand shaking a baby bottle, the trickle of milk splashing against the inside of Detta's wrist. But was it memory that made Eva see Detta's narrow, slightly equine face between the ruffles of the curtains in the dark? Or was it only because she had found a photograph of the two of them: Eva, ridiculously small but recognizable by the dark fringe of scraggly hair across her forehead, sitting on a shaggy toy bear on wheels; Detta behind her, her dark nurse's veil falling to her gaunt shoulders; and behind both of them the white pillars of the Staatstheater. She could never be certain; nor could she tell if it was remembrance that made her see Detta lean over the white-painted bars of the crib where she had slept in those days.

"*Auf Wiedersehen*, little Eva. Detta is going away. *Nach Amerika.* . . ."

Perhaps she merely pieced the scene together from words overheard, things told to her by others. Anna, their cook, still spoke of Detta now and then—how possessive she had been of Eva; how she had ruled the household with a despot's will: taking over, ordering Frau Bentheim and Anna about, even forbidding Eva to climb onto her mother's lap for a good morning kiss—rank jealousy disguised as concern that she might pick up a sore throat along with a bit of parental affection.

"Luckily, her sister fell ill and she left," Anna said heartlessly, slamming pot lids on the stove as if to banish the irksome ghost of Detta's presence. "Though, between you and me, Eva, the sister was just an excuse. It was a husband she hoped to find in America, the Land of Opportunities." And Anna laughed, not pleasantly, putting her hands on her trim hips.

Be that as it may, Detta did find a husband: her sister's widower, whom she married within six months of her sister's demise. That winter, perhaps as a final gesture of parting, a cardboard box pasted with foreign stamps arrived for Fräulein Eva Bentheim. Inside was a rustling red taffeta dress with lacy collar and cuffs and a little card with a flower border, which said: *Christmas Greetings from Overseas.* And, strangely, whenever Eva felt the swish of the taffeta skirt against her knees, she could hear the cool linen rustle of Detta's veil in that dimly remembered, tearful farewell across the white bars of her crib.

Though Detta's dress had come at Christmas, their own holiday was Hanukkah. There was no tree at the Bentheims', as there was at the Haeberles' upstairs. Instead, candles were lit on a silver menorah, and afterward her mother sat down at the piano and she and Eva would sing, with her father listening quietly from *his* chair and her grandfather impatiently from *his*. (Neither her father nor her grandfather knew how to sing, but her father liked to listen to music.) Then her mother would play the melody once more, without singing the words—play it very softly on the topmost scales of the piano. It sounded muted and tinkly, like the chimes on the Rathaus tower . . . .

On some evenings of the eight nights of Hanukkah, Eva went upstairs to be with her cousins Ella and Uschi for the lighting of the candles. She felt needed there, for upstairs nobody knew how to sing: neither Ella nor Uschi nor Aunt Gustl. And certainly not Uncle Ludwig, who, unlike his brother, didn't even care to *hear* music. And since nobody played the piano either, Eva would sing at the top of her voice to help her cousins stay on key, feeling quite indispensable.

But one evening, after Uschi had blithely spoiled an especially lovely phrase with a particularly jarring note, she put a cautioning finger to her lips and waved Eva aside.

"Ella told Mother to make you stop *screaming!*" Uschi whispered. "She doesn't think it suits the song, Eva. Don't you know what it is about?"

In truth, Eva had never given any thought to it. It was the melody she had enjoyed, and the intriguing sequence of sounds in a language that was, her father had told her, the ancient language of the Bible.

"What *is* it about?" she asked in a low voice so that Ella would not overhear and burst into the room with a gleeful, "You *seeee!*"

"Why, it's about the brave Maccabees," Uschi said. "About a kind of miracle. And an evil tyrant. It all happened a very long time ago."

"And *now*, Uschi? Could miracles still happen today?" It seemed a fascinating possibility.

Uschi wrinkled her freckled brow. "I don't know," she said uncertainly. "I've never heard of one to happen." She blinked her green eyes in concentration and shrugged. "Perhaps it is because there aren't any more evil tyrants."

Eva would have been lost without Uschi—and without Ella, too, trying as she might be at times. Downstairs, there was only herself and the grown-ups. She was always a hapless One against her cousins' invincible Twosomeness —a humiliating state exploited by Aunt Gustl, who frequently shut the door in Eva's face with a curt: "The girls have gone out and won't be back till dinner!"

"I wish *I* had a sister!" she told Anna as she crept into the kitchen to let her outraged pride be soothed by a crust of Anna's freshly baked pie.

Anna laughed. She was a buxom, trim-waisted girl, and when she tilted her head the way she did now, with the honey-blond braids primly coiled over each ear, Eva thought her very pretty. It was a judgment she kept well hidden from Anna, for fear she might turn vain and flirtatious, like Aunt Gustl's cook, and go on Sunday outings with strange men and, perhaps, even get married and leave.

"I've told you before to put a piece of sugar on your window sill for the stork, Eva, but you never do as you're told!"

That evening, after dinner, Eva stealthily took two sugar cubes from the bowl on the dining-room table and hid them in her pocket. Two, in case one might slip off the sill and drop to the street below, and stealthily, because Anna's advice was always accompanied by an amused laugh, raising suspicions about its validity. If the sugar was worth a try at all—and anything was, really, in her situation—it was best to go about it secretly, taking no chances of ridicule until Anna's suggestion had been put to the test. Again and again, that night, she stole out of bed and peered through the curtains to make sure the sweet white bait was still there. In the morning, she remembered it the moment she woke up. She ran to the window and threw back the curtains with a thumping heart. But it had rained during the night, and the little cubes had melted in a syrupy stain on the glistening iron sill. . . .

She might have tried again, had it not been for something she overheard Ella tell her girl friends that very afternoon. They were picking dandelions on the lawn of the town park and gossipping about Trude, a "new" girl from one of the cities to the north who had at once soared to the top of Ella's class.

"Trude may think she is very smart," Ella said with a shrug. "But there is still a thing or two she doesn't know!"

And they all looked at one another and giggled, and suddenly Ella turned her head and looked straight at Eva—a cool and knowing look (had she seen the melted sugar on the windowsill?)—until Eva began to giggle too in sheer confusion, giggling harder than any of them, without knowing why.

After that, she never spoke to Anna about having a sister anymore, and in time she also stopped nagging her mother. Her mother had not teased her the way Anna had, but Eva knew she did not like to be asked.

"Perhaps someday, Eva—someday, perhaps," her mother would say, turning her face away and patting her hair in place.

Only once her mother had said "perhaps" in a different way, and had bent down awkwardly, heavily, to kiss Eva's cheek. She wore a yellow dress that day, gathered in tiny pleats at the bodice, and when she stooped to kiss Eva, the pleats opened like a fan and spread around her waist. But that evening, her mother had not come to the dinner table, and there had been a gloomy, silent meal alone with her father and grandfather. Her mother stayed in bed for an endless number of days, it seemed to Eva, and when she got up again, she was wan and thin and even more quiet than usual. Eva hardly dared touch her, much less upset her with her old complaint.

Every afternoon Aunt Cora came in from Reinberg to take Eva for a walk so that her mother could rest. Afterward, her mother and Aunt Cora sat in the living room and spoke in low tones, stirring their coffees absently and forgetting to drink them. Eva played in her own room, leaving the door ajar so she could listen, while she pretended not to by noisily banging her toys.

"But you are still so young, Martha," Aunt Cora was saying, nodding her head emphatically so that a stray black ringlet escaped from the thick knot of hair at the nape of her neck. "Perhaps someday—you must not give up hope."

Eva's mother gazed into her lap and said nothing. The lamp above the table shed a soft light on her brown hair. "Perhaps it is better this way, Cora," she said at last, "with Jonas' health so precarious—and the times. . . ."

It was the first time Eva heard someone say "the times" in that troubled, foreboding way in which she would hear it said again and again in the days to come.

But that evening, when her mother helped her get ready for bed, Eva knew only that her mother was sad, and she wished there were something she might do to make her smile. She could tell her that she loved her, of course; but it seemed at once too little and too much to do so. All children loved their mothers; it was as natural to love your mother as it was to love the bed you slept in, the street where you played, the town where you were born. Eva wished there might be a special reason she could name for loving *hers*, but she could think of none. It would have been easy with everyone else: her father because he was wise, Uncle Lutz because he made people laugh, her mother's two sisters because they were beautiful. But her mother was simply her mother, dear to her for herself alone.

Later, after her mother had sat on the edge of her bed for a moment before turning off the light, Eva closed her eyes and listened to the murmur of voices from the living room. There was her father's serious voice and his brother Ludwig's skeptical one in reply, Aunt Gustl's heavy Bavarian accent, and Aunt Cora's mischievous laughter. Only her mother's voice was missing from those of the others in the next room. Perhaps she was still in the kitchen, whipping cream for the waffles she had baked; perhaps she sat quietly under the lamp at the round table, doing some intricate needlework with broad, winter-roughened hands. All the ladies knitted or crocheted or embroidered; but her mother's large, capable hands seemed better suited for gardening or kneading bread than for the delicate handwork ladies must do. Yet her mother was neither forceful enough to oppose custom nor agile enough to evade it; and so her fingers had learned to fashion an interminable succession of pretty, superfluous things. Every linen tablecloth was crisscrossed with finely stitched patterns, every sofa pillow crocheted in fluffy wool; the earthenware teapot had its yellow cozy, the silver coffee urn came swathed in midnight blue.

"Martha does have a way with color," Aunt Hanni would say airily, glancing at her own carefully groomed hands lying in poised idleness in her lap.

Eva's Aunt Hanni—her father's elder sister—did have the courage to defy convention; she felt no obligation to join the ladies in their sewing or their murmured talk of recipes and shopping tours.

"Cooking is such a waste of time," she would say, folding her arms under her bosom with a shrug. "And until Stefan graduates from the university, I cannot afford new clothes." With that, she would edge her chair out of the busy circle of the women toward the smoke-bound group of the men and join their conversation.

"No, Ludwig, it is more than a question of alleviating hardship," Eva heard her tell her brother. "Unless the economic crisis is resolved, it will be the end of the Republic."

The end of the Republic? Eva wondered what it meant. Perhaps it had to do with "the times" of which her mother had spoken, or with the war that had ended before Eva was born but was still talked about as if it had never ended at all. Perhaps it was about the men who were out of work and sat on benches in the park, their idle hands thrust into the frayed pockets of their coats. People were always talking about things in big words that Eva could not understand. Yet tonight, even though she could not understand, there was something in the drift of their voices that made her afraid.

The door opened softly, and her mother came into the room. She bent over Eva's bed and tugged the eiderdown quilt over her arms. The fire in the little stove had died down, and the room had grown chilly.

Her mother smelled of her baking, mixed with a faint scent of sachet. She never rouged her lips; there was no need to wipe one's cheek surreptitiously after a kiss, as with Aunt Cora. And her mother never discreetly slipped out of a hug, the way Aunt Hanni did when her hair was carefully waved and arranged for a special occasion.

Her mother's rough-gentle hands slipped over Eva's forehead. Since her tonsils had begun to give her trouble, Eva frequently caught her mother touching her fingers to her forehead and scanning her face with a searching look. Somehow, even with her eyes closed, she knew this was how her mother was looking at her now, and she felt safe and warm and watched over.

Suddenly, she wished she could open her eyes and tell her mother that she knew why she loved her. But she had already fallen asleep.

3 ✲✲✲

Most evenings after supper, Aunt Gustl and Uncle Ludwig stopped by for a visit with Grandfather over coffee and cake. Eva's mother, always needlessly flustered over the state of her housekeeping, would fluff the sofa pillows and set out fresh ash trays.

"Still busy, Martha? Tsk, tsk!" Aunt Gustl would cluck in mock commiseration. "My, my, we're all dolled up tonight, aren't we?"

Aunt Gustl, to be sure, was *always* ready; Eva's mother foolishly mistook her willingness to cut corners for efficiency, and the reference to her own tardiness stung all the more. Nor could Aunt Gustl be accused of "dolling up." A darkly pretty woman whose face and figure had been allowed to grow plump from an overfondness for sweets, she favored matronly shirtwaist dresses in somber colors, with a bit of tea-tinted lace at the throat. For a long time, before Eva had become clever enough to tell crepe from cotton and black from navy blue, she was under the mistaken impression that, summer or winter, Aunt Gustl's wardrobe consisted of a single dress.

Like her kisses which bristled faintly from the telltale traces of a streak of fuzz on her upper lip, Aunt Gustl's infrequent praise unfailingly prickled with an underbrush of thorns.

"Eva, that was a nice card you sent the girls from your grandparents' last week," she said on one occasion. "But your *handwriting*—tsk! tsk! What is it they keep in their inkwells in Ettingen—mud?"

Eva, red-faced, forced a grin, swallowing the smart retort that was on the tip of her tongue. It was not too high a price to pay for permission to play with her cousins. For their sake she had learned to comply humbly with their mother's rules and conditions, to manage an ingratiating giggle over Aunt Gustl's banter, which was as heavy as the Bavarian *knödel* in her soups.

"May I go upstairs and do my homework with the girls, Aunt Gustl?" she asked. And at her aunt's somewhat belated nod and her admonition "but no games until Ella has finished studying for her French exam!" Eva hurried to her desk to gather her things.

Upstairs, in the little study off their bedroom, her cousins already sat over their books at the round table under the purple ceiling lamp. They greeted Eva warmly, moving their school things with only a trace of reluctance at having to make room for hers. Eva opened her Swabian history book and began to read about the Hohenstaufen kings, whose medieval reign as Holy Roman Emperors seemed closer to the heart of Fräulein Fink, her teacher, than the wavering fortunes of their embattled republican government in Berlin. Ella was conjugating French verbs with a scowl; Uschi, with enviable neatness and precision, shaded in blue rivers, brown mountains, and green lowlands on a pencil-drawn map of South Germany in her geography book.

When they had finished their homework, Ella offered to play "Chopsticks" with Eva on the clinky upright in the corner that Ella had recently, and wisely, abandoned in favor of drawing lessons. Then Uschi suggested a round of Aggravation, brought out the board and the dice, and let Eva choose her favorite red tokens. Ella won, as usual, but promised a return match for another night. When it was time to leave—Grandfather had made it an unofficial rule that children should be in their own apartments and, preferably, in their beds by nine thirty—Eva considered it an evening well spent. Running into the Upstairs in the staircase, she was able to wish Aunt Gustl a sincerely grateful Good Night.

Being Aunt Gustl's niece, after all, had certain advantages, too. Eva's mother, from her own small-town youth in the Swabian countryside a firm believer in fresh air and exercise, made sure that Eva had an abundance of both.

"Because it's *good* for you!" was her cheerful reply to Eva's repeated "Oh, why do I have to?"

"Because it will make you grow tall and strong!"

And, in their seasons, she took Eva swimming in the Neckar, ice-skating on the pond in the park, and on long brisk walks through the wooded hills above Thalstadt. "Breathe deep!" she would say, taking deep breaths herself and sending encouraging smiles in Eva's direction. Eva was skeptical of it all; aside from her tonsils, she seemed healthy enough, and neither sunshine on her bare arms and legs nor oxygen in her obligingly expanding lungs made her grow noticeably taller. But they were close and happy afternoons: the long walks, especially, through the rustling leaves, in the crisp, bright October air.

Eva's mother was not an articulate woman; she did not read many books, her wisdom was not drawn from the printed page. Rather, it seemed to spring from life itself, from the outdoors she loved and celebrated in song. Music was her mother's expression; she had a warm mezzo-soprano voice and an inexhaustible fund of songs for every season and every mood. On those walks Eva came to know Schubert and Mozart and the simple beauty of folksongs —songs about love and farewell, violets and linden trees, happiness and hurt. And she discovered, miraculously, that their voices—her mother's full, sure one and her thinner, tentative one—blended and entwined, complementing and enhancing one another, merging into a new and perfect unity. It was called *harmony*, her mother said.

But as the afternoons grew shorter and the skies bleaker, Eva began to long for the warmer, lazier pleasures Aunt Gustl provided for *her* daughters. On the way home through the dusky streets with their wintry smell of burning leaves, she had envious visions of her cousins' brown heads bent close together over a game of Aggravation and afterward a pot of steaming cocoa and *Gugelhopf* cake.

"When we get home, Mother, may I go upstairs for a little while?"

And at her Mother's reluctant nod (was it really concern that Eva might "fill up on sweets and spoil her supper" or was it a twinge of jealousy?), Eva rudely abandoned her mother at their door and ran upstairs to ring Aunt Gustl's bell.

At once there was a burst of laughter and the shuffle of slippered feet on the rug.

"My, what a surprise!" Aunt Gustl said, holding the

door ajar for a fearful moment of suspense before admitting her to the gay and fragrant paradise beyond. "We hardly expected the honor anymore today. Your mother must've marched you as far as Nuremberg and back!"

And putting her chubby hand on Eva's neck, as if she were a repentant fugitive safely retrieved, she led her into her cousins' room.

The low lamp with its purple beads and fringes shone brightly on Uschi's and Ella's faces; the smell of cocoa was irresistible; and on the table—just beyond the assembled tokens set up for another round of Aggravation—was a last piece of iced and raisin-studded *Gugelhopf!*

Yes, being Aunt Gustl's niece did have its compensations.

4 ✝✝✝

Though Eva skated, swam, walked, and swallowed her daily ration of cod liver oil, she remained small. In her father's bookstore, the penciled notches on the doorpost by which he hopefully charted her progress crept upward only by reluctant millimeters; and from season to season she barely grew into her clothes, let alone out of them.

"I wouldn't worry about it, Eva," her father said, snapping his mechanical pencil shut with an air of determined nonchalance. "It really doesn't matter. Not for a girl, anyway," he added ruefully.

"Even if I were a boy," Eva said loyally, "I wouldn't want to be tall. I want to be like you."

Her father smiled, pleased. "Don't let that stop you from growing. It's what's *inside* people that counts, not what they look like."

It sounded dubious. If that was so, why was her father so concerned about her lack of height, so self-conscious of his own? It was true that people sometimes said one thing and did another, but she had never known her father to be guilty of this puzzling adult sin. It was all very perplexing.

Aunt Hanni, her father's older sister, was also small, but

she carried her diminutive body, so much like one of the dainty Meissen figurines in the alcove of her living room, with a self-assurance much like Grandfather's. And this despite the fact that Aunt Hanni had "not had an easy life," as Eva's mother would say from time to time, sympathetically but without further elaboration.

It was from Ella, under a pledge of secrecy, that Eva learned more. Aunt Hanni's marriage to Uncle Poldi, entered into at the urging of Grandfather who feared his aloof and studious daughter would turn into a "bluestocking," had been less than ideal. Uncle Poldi, whom Eva remembered only as a benignly moon-faced presence over her crib, had not been *serieuse*, as Ella had heard the grown-ups say; he was a blustering, happy-go-lucky fellow, out of his depth with his reserved and cultivated wife. And before the inflation wiped out his haphazardly run business, Ella went on to report with even greater secrecy, Uncle Poldi had been "a bit of a high liver," with an appetite for good food and wine, and a gleam in his eye for the ladies.

Aunt Hanni, too intelligent to remain unaware of this and too proud to acknowledge it, had suffered in silence without availing herself of even a sister-in-law's shoulder to cry on. When Uncle Poldi died suddenly, Aunt Hanni was left with a son to raise and educate on what was left after paying off Uncle Poldi's debts—but with her sense of dignity restored at last. Refusing help from her brothers, she supplemented her modest income by doing French translations at the corner desk in her living room and accepted assistance from Grandfather only for Stefan's tuition at Heidelberg University.

Since Aunt Hanni was alone most of the time, with only Hexle, her calico cat, for company, Eva tried to visit her as often as she could. Sometimes she would visit with Uschi; they would sit on the carpet and leaf through Aunt Hanni's pearl-gray family album while Hexle darted sleek-furred from below the green plush sofa and flitted away again before they could manage to pet her.

Eva and Uschi loved the satin-bound album with its vanished world of people who were at once familiar and strangers. Here was Grandfather as a clear-eyed young man, with the young wife on his arm wearing a bustled, wasp-waisted suit and the same plumed hat that now hung on the stand in the attic. Here were their fathers and Aunt Hanni transformed into shy-faced children. Dressed in the lace-trimmed, loose-fitting clothes that children wore in faded old photos, they sat on, or leaned against the beautiful wooden rocking-horse that later was owned in turn by Stefan, by Ella, and by Uschi—but which had finally, its glossy finish scuffed and pealed, broken apart and been put out to pasture, to Eva's rankling regret.

A few pages farther on, there was Aunt Hanni in her wedding gown, tiny and with her hair still brown and elaborately arranged under the bridal veil. Next to her was Uncle Poldi, a large, full-chested gentleman with a rakish mustache. He was already showing signs of that corpulence which became more and more pronounced on the following pages and which, Uschi whispered, had finally contributed to his untimely death. And there was Stefan: Stefan as a round-eyed, round-bottomed baby flopped on the inevitable bearskin; Stefan in his white sailor suit, walking at his mother's hand in the park; Stefan with books under his arm at the gate of the Gymnasium grounds; and Stefan in his ribboned university student's cap, standing beside the famous Heidelberg Fass, the giant wine barrel in the cellar of Heidelberg Castle.

Stefan, Stefan, Stefan. It occurred to Eva that Aunt Hanni, who could talk politics with the men and did translations instead of needlework, was just like any other mother when it came to her son. Perhaps that was what people were like: differing in shapes and sizes, feelings and thoughts, and yet very much the same when it came to certain things—loving their children, for instance, and wanting them to be happy and safe. Not very much could go wrong with her world, it seemed to Eva, as long as this remained true.

5 ❦❦❦

One thing that Eva longed for was a garden. Grandfather's house stood in the busy center of town, across from the Crown Apothecary and the big round clock of Roeblin's watch store. All day long there was the clang of the streetcar rounding the curving tracks of the square, the blare of impatient automobiles, and the rumble of wagons bringing vegetables and fruits to the nearby Marktplatz. But at night, when the city slept, the peal of the chimes on the Rathaus tower came clearly across the rooftops and drifted into her small room.

Lacking a garden, she played with Uschi on the worn cobblestones of the *Gässle*, the sleepy old street behind Grandfather's house that time and city haste had somehow passed by. They played quiet games, because the *Gässle* was a quiet place. The people who lived in the little slate-roofed houses were old, and their children had grown up and moved away. When Uschi and Eva curtsied and said *"Grüss Gott,"* they smiled in return; but their smiles drooped like the dusty geraniums in their windowboxes. Perhaps they were lonely and forgotten, like the *Gässle* itself.

The house across from theirs was a prim house, though its roof sagged a bit and its front step creaked when Uschi and Eva skipped from its stoop. It belonged to the Muenzers, an elderly couple who always walked arm in arm. When they happened to meet Eva on the *Gässle*, Frau Muenzer always paused to inquire about Grandfather's health. But she seemed especially pleased whenever she met Eva's father.

While Eva impatiently shuffled her feet, her father and Frau Muenzer would talk earnestly for many slow minutes, oblivious of the furtive tug of Eva's hand on her father's sleeve. She gathered that they were speaking of old times, days of her father's youth. But though they often smiled and nodded in remembrance, their voices and their smiles were curiously remote, as if they feared to delve too deeply into that bygone past they shared.

"Why does Frau Muenzer call you 'son,' Father?" she asked one day, as if the word were a key that in its turning might unlock a door.

For a moment she thought he had not heard her.

"Frau Muenzer's son, Karl, was my boyhood friend, Eva," he said at last. "We went to school together, played together on the *Gässle*, even went into the army on the same day."

"Does Karl have children? Does he ever bring them to see his parents?"

Her father gazed across the cobblestones, toward the house with the sagging front stoop. "Karl never came home from the war, Eva. He died in France as a soldier."

She stared at him, shocked. Why had she asked, why had he answered? Always now, when she saw the two old neighbors, she would think of their dead son, lying in a cold, distant earth, forever gone from the lonely house across the street.

"I *hate* the French!" she cried in a choked voice, clenching her fists and burying her face in the roughness of her father's coat.

But he tilted her chin gently and shook his head. "Never think such thoughts again, Eva," he said quietly. "It is only war we must hate, not the poor people on either side who do the dying."

Perhaps she did not understand it all. But the first seed of understanding was planted there, on the *Gässle*, where the sparse grass sprouted stubbornly between the cobble-stones.

So much that was wise and good, it seemed to her in those days, came to her from her father. He was that kind of man. She knew it in her own childish way, and others, grown-ups, acknowledged it in theirs. If they happened to be flippant people, like Uncle Lutz, her mother's brother, they were at times impatient with his deep seriousness and sensibility. Behind her father's back, Uncle Lutz had nicknamed his sister's husband "The Saint"—and though Eva regarded the name as apt and even complimentary, her ears were fine enough to catch the irreverent note of a family joke.

"Jonas," Uncle Lutz said another time, as always well beyond her father's hearing, "Jonas considers the world his personal Nineveh, doomed to the Lord's wrath lest it mend its wicked ways and listen to his preaching."

Aunt Cora laughed, dark ringlets dancing at the nape of her neck. Alfred, Cora's tall, debonair husband with the craggy face and the perennially well-chosen tie, smiled his surprisingly gentle smile. Even Uncle Ludwig bit his lip, his owlish, skeptical features mellowed indulgently; he, too, was always chiding his brother for looking at the world through dark glasses.

Only her mother indignantly shook her head. "Jonas never preaches, you know that, Lutz," she said reproachfully. "And if the world were a little kinder, we might all sleep easier for it."

Uncle Lutz winked at his audience. "Has anyone ever heard Martha disagree with her husband? After a dozen years of marriage, she is still the adoring bride. Shall I tell you what kind of bride my sister was? On her first wedding anniversary, she told the family in Ettingen: 'You know, Jonas has no faults whatever!' "

Now even her mother could not keep from laughing. But Aunt Cora gave her brother a significant stare and said with a sidelong glance at Eva: "Enough, Lutz! *Kinder haben lange Ohren!*"

Long ears or not, Eva had heard every word of it. And for once Uncle Lutz's talent for making people laugh seemed less than admirable to her, because the laughter had been at her father's expense. There was a fierce, almost jealous quality in the way Eva felt about her father—a quality of protectiveness that no one else called up in her, because no one else seemed in need of it. Her father's physical frailness and delicate health were only part of the reason. Young as she was, Eva sensed an *inner* vulnerability that left him defenseless against a world he saw so clearly, experienced so keenly, and felt himself so powerless to influence or change.

In his own life, too, it seemed to Eva, things had not

turned out exactly the way her father once had hoped. Why, for instance, had he become a businessman like his father and brother when she knew that he had really wanted to teach literature at a university? She needed no one to tell her, as family friends often did, that her father was a highly intelligent man. Nor did she need to be reminded on numerous occasions by Aunt Hanni that in his youth her father had attended the Gymnasium, Thalstadt's outstanding preparatory school, where he had studied Latin and Greek in addition to modern languages and literature. It was during his senior year at the Gymnasium that Jonas Bentheim's essay, "The Idea of Freedom in German Classical Drama" (an enviously awesome title!), had won the graduating class's Schiller Prize. "And he, a *Jewish* schoolboy!" Aunt Hanni always added, with satisfaction.

The Schiller Prize—a thick, maroon-bound volume of the poet-playwright's collected works—still occupied an honored position on the bookshelves in the Bentheim drawing room. But her father's hopes of teaching literature after obtaining his diploma from Munich University had gone unfulfilled.

Eva knew that it had to do with the World War, of which she had heard her father speak often since that first time when she had asked him about Karl. Like Karl, her father, then a university student, had been sent to the Western front—an unlikely soldier, slight and looking ill at ease in the stiff, field-gray uniform in the photo on the album page, from which he gazed out gravely and questioningly behind his rimless glasses.

It was a war he considered "a tragedy—for Europe, for Germany"—a war deplored by so many of the great literary figures, German and French, he deeply admired. Yet in the end, he would add sadly, most had "capitulated, caught the war fever—they, the moral leadership of Europe, the conscience of their time."

"If there had been a real opposition on both sides," he said one day, implying, Eva felt, that he, too, would have been among it. "But then," he continued in a troubled voice, "If one loves one's country, is called upon to serve it, can there be circumstances when one is justified in refusing?"

Then Eva found out how much her father's life had been changed by the war.

"My brother hasn't had a well moment since he came home from the war," Aunt Hanni said bitterly one winter afternoon when Eva stopped by on her roller skates and answered the usual inquiry about her family by saying her father had been in pain.

"Did your father ever tell you he was practically dragged from a hospital bed into the army, after a serious operation? A sick boy, carrying all that heavy equipment, having to throw himself down on the damp ground for rifle training and drills, on his stomach that had just been sewn up and never had a chance to heal properly!"

Aunt Hanni quickly dabbed her eyes and nose with the back of her wrist—she who always carried a dainty handkerchief and was usually so elegant and composed. Embarrassed, Eva shrank into the billowing cushions of the sofa and busied herself by ruffling and smoothing the deep-green plush with her fingers. She felt vaguely uncomfortable listening to her aunt tell things about her father that he

obviously preferred to keep to himself, whether to protect
Eva or his own privacy. And there was something wrong
about the image she perceived of him through someone
else's eyes, however loving and well-meaning. It was as if
she were looking at her father through her mother's
pearl-handled opera glasses, seeing him by turns larger and
smaller than she knew him to be.

Aunt Hanni was pouring homemade eggnog into two
tiny smoked glasses as she would for an adult visitor,
though she filled Eva's glass barely enough for a taste—"or
your father will scold me for sending you home *schicker!*"

Schicker was a Jewish expression meaning "tipsy," and it
sounded funny coming from Aunt Hanni, who rarely used
the homey turns of speech with which Eva's relatives in
Ettingen—her mother's family—freely salted their conversations.

Eva laughed, relieved that her aunt seemed to have
regained her composure. "It will keep me warm on the way
home!"

But she was in no hurry to go. Aunt Hanni's living room
with its trailing ferns and faded pictures in their oval
frames—and with Hexle darting between them without
upsetting a single one—was one of her favorite places.
Sipping the thick, yolk-colored treat, she let her eyes
wander over the Meissen figurines and miniature ivory
furniture on the glass-enclosed shelves in the alcove.

"When Jonas went back to Munich after his medical
discharge at the end of the war, his health was gone and so
were his hopes of teaching." Aunt Hanni's voice abruptly
brought Eva back from the small, self-contained world
behind the glass. "The universities were 'hotbeds of
dissension,' as the newspapers put it—monarchists versus

defenders of the young Republic, nationalists versus sup-
porters of the League of Nations. And those who stood for
peace, for democracy, bore the brunt of it, including
beatings and worse. My brother, in addition, was a Jew.
And a sick man," Aunt Hanni finished, in the same bitter
tone in which she had begun the conversation.

"I think I'd better go now," Eva mumbled, wriggling out
from the velvety depths of the sofa.

Aunt Hanni walked with her to the door.

"A sick man," she repeated, handing Eva her roller
skates. "A brilliant man, with a fine career cut short, selling
books in his father's store!"

"Well, he *likes* selling books," Eva said, in a voice that
sounded shrill to her own ears. "And he *isn't* a sick man,"
she called back over her shoulder from halfway down the
stairs. "Only *sometimes*."

But Aunt Hanni was closing her door and probably
hadn't heard.

Her father was still in the bookstore when Eva looked in to
remind him that it was time for supper. He was checking
an order of newly arrived art books, handling the linen-
bound volumes expertly, even tenderly, leafing through the
glossy pages with the same animation she had seen on his
face during a spirited conversation with one of his friends.
He looked contented enough, she reassured herself.

"Would you like to shelve these, Eva?" He pushed a stack
of brightly jacketed books down the counter in her
direction. "I've reordered *Emil and the Detectives*—you're
not the only Erich Kästner fan in Thalstadt!"

Putting her current favorite on the shelf in the children's

section, Eva daydreamed about being Emil's spunky cousin
Pony, who rode all over Berlin on her bicycle to help Emil
and the gang capture the sinister Man in the Stiff Hat.

Well, no such luck for her! Her father refused to let her
ride a bicycle in the city, and the boys in her class weren't
likely to let a girl help them catch anyone.

Besides, no one sinister ever came to Thalstadt.

With a sudden surge of relief she watched her father put
the last of the new books on the shelves and shut the door to
his office for the night. Here he was safe, in Grandfather's
house and store, surrounded by his books and with no one
to bother him or hurt him—"or worse." Why anyone
should feel such hatred toward her father or others like him
she could not imagine; but Aunt Hanni had been serious
enough when she spoke about it to make it plain that such
things had happened, could happen again.

But not in Thalstadt, she told herself once more, waiting
on the landing to let her father catch up with her. Upstairs,
her mother met them at the door with a smile at seeing
them arrive together and asked nothing more extraordinary
of Eva than that she put her roller skates where they
belonged and wash her hands before supper.

6 ❦❦❦

The year was round, like an apple, endlessly circular and reassuring in its unvarying familiarity. And, like an apple, it had two layers—a smooth yet robust outer one and another one underneath, more vulnerable in texture and peculiarly one's own.

The outside year was the year of the red calendar at school. It was Everyone's Year, with its school and vacation weeks immutably fixed, its daily alternation of study and play, homework and grades—and tantalizingly ahead, the long, sun-filled summer interlude of seemingly unending freedom. And then, abruptly, one was back in the cool, strangely unreal confines of the classroom, with books freshly wrapped in sturdy brown covers, pencils sharpened to extravagant points, voices a little too loud, laughter a little too bold, and a thumping, expectant, uneasy heart.

Everyone's Year entered brashly and noisily on Sylvester night, when fireworks crackled against the midwinter sky and grown-ups stayed out to celebrate until the gray hours of the New Year. Eva would take advantage of the situation by sleeping at her cousins' upstairs, where Ella treated the two younger girls to a midnight sip of mulled wine and told ghost stories in the dark by the gleam of a green-clothed flashlight, while they stifled screams of terror and delight by pulling the bed covers over their heads.

Interspersed through the year were other special days, like beads on a long string of weeks. There was *Fasching*, in February, with its carnival fun and children's costume parties; Easter, when Anna wore her new hat and gloves to church, leaving a basket of blue-speckled eggs under the Gramophone for Eva to find; the Autumn Fair on the Neckar, where she and Renate, her best friend at school, rode little red cars that bumped into one another under a shower of sparks and the squeals of their occupants.

And there was Christmas, when Eva and her cousins —asked in to admire the Haeberles' candlelit tree with its shimmering globes and spun-silver "angels' hair"—stood shyly in the subtly transformed room and gazed at the blazing alien candle glow with envyless appreciation, from courteous, unswayed eyes.

For was there not, beneath the bright and busy year they shared with their neighbors and schoolmates, another, less visible, parallel year of their own? A year with its *own* holidays and their *own* customs and symbols: the candles of Hanukkah in their eight-branched menorah; the Purim play, in March, about Queen Esther who was as brave as she was beautiful; Passover with her grandparents in Ettingen, where Grandfather Weil filled an extra cup of wine for the Prophet Elijah, leaving the front door ajar; the Feast of Tabernacles in October, when Rabbi Gideon offered thanksgivings outdoors in a bower hung with harvest fruits and vegetables, and everyone partook of the holiday wine and plaited challah bread that tasted nowhere better than in this leafy, fragrant place. . . .

This year, their own, began in early fall, with Rosh Hashonoh, the Hebrew New Year's Day that was at once festive and solemn, followed by Yom Kippur, an even holier day of fasting and repentance. On the evenings that ushered in these Days of Awe, Eva's cousins would call for her after dinner on their way to the synagogue. Ahead of their parents they would walk briskly through the unaccustomed chill of the early dusk, past Herr Loeser's shuttered flower shop and through the narrow arcade of the Evangelical Art Gallery, where stylized portraits with slender New Testament hands gestured wanly above trailing sleeves.

The synagogue, under its blue and golden cupola, was crowded with holiday faces and finery. Ella trudged upstairs to the balcony to sit with her mother in the women's section. Eva and Uschi walked past the somber-clad rows of the men and slipped into the girls' benches that faced the Ark containing the Scrolls of the Law. The richly embroidered velvet curtain was already drawn to reveal the gold-crowned Torah scrolls in their crimson, silver-shot mantles—like bright and cherished children of the house brought out to delight the guests on a festive occasion. The organ soared, the choir sang with fervor. Eva could hear her mother's fine mezzo-soprano join in the singing and followed her lead, fitting the scarcely understood Hebrew words to the familiar holiday airs. Next to her, Lilo Levi poked Eva's arm behind her opened prayer book, casting a meaningful glance across the aisle, where the unruly boys from their Hebrew class fidgeted under the dignity and discomfort of holiday collars and ties.

The cantor in his flowing robe raised the filled *kiddush* cup to chant the benediction, his voice sparkling darkly, like the red wine within its circling silver rim. Then the shofar, the ancient ram's horn, sounded its piercing call for repentance, primordial and plaintive as the cry of a wounded maternal beast bleating for its strayed young. Rabbi Gideon, bearded and gaunt, lifted his scholar's hands above the pulpit. He called on God to forgive their sins of the past year and spoke the priestly blessing over their bowed heads: "and may the Lord turn His Countenance upon thee and give thee Peace"—but not before he had wisely asked God's guidance for President Hindenburg, "that venerable aged man who stands at the helm of our state. . . ."

Leaving the synagogue arm in arm with her parents —her father, an infrequent worshipper, carrying his folded prayer shawl and looking self-consciously handsome in his ceremonial top hat—Eva felt wrapped as securely in the rabbi's blessing as in an impenetrable cloak.

Outside, in the lamplit street, friends and families clustered briefly, shaking hands and murmuring, "May you be inscribed for a Good Year." And somewhere above the familiar cupola dimly outlined against the autumnal Swabian sky, God listened, Eva knew, and entered their names in the Book of Life with a benevolent flourish of His hand—the way her father signed her report card, knowing she could have done better, trusting she *would*, next year.

It was one of the special things about their "own" year with its procession of holidays to come, this feeling that God was close by, all-knowing, all-forgiving—even if one was not especially good, and not at all "religious." God, the remote God of the spired churches, was their ancestral, very human God—angry sometimes, often sad, but always reachable, part of the family. It made it easy to be *both*—Jewish and Swabian, Swabian Jews—as natural as it was for the apple to have two layers, one fitting comfortably inside the other, neither complete without the other, but together forming an integral, delicious whole.

"What better place to be a child than in Thalstadt," her father said one afternoon, meeting her unexpectedly at the streetcar stop on her return from school and taking the long way home under the chestnut trees of the Schlossplatz.

And she, shrugging off the note of unease that edged his complacent words, would not have exchanged Thalstadt —her house, her school, her park, her synagogue—for any place in the world.

PART · TWO

Seeds of Storm

1 ♣♣♣

Waking, she heard the fading sound of rain like the subdued rise and fall of voices. She had gone to sleep with the murmur of voices in her ears—voices in the next room, talking late into the night. Yesterday had been Election Day for Reichspresident, and the grown-ups had stayed up to listen to the radio as the early returns began to trickle in. "Politics is not for children," her mother had said, and had sent her off to bed.

For a while, lying in the dark at the thin edge of sleep, Eva had listened idly to the polished, disembodied radio voice beyond the door and tried to fix the places it ticked off on an imaginary map spread out against her bedroom wall: East Prussian fishing villages on the Baltic Sea, towns with familiar Swabian names along the Neckar River, dusty coal regions of the Ruhr, and distant Hansa cities in the North.

"*Sozialdemokraten*," the pointedly impartial voice went on, ". . . *Nationalsozialisten . . . Kommunisten. . . .*"

The Communists wore red armbands, and when two of them met in the street, they bent their arms at the elbow and made a fist. The National Socialists, the Nazis, wore swastikas on their brown uniforms and said "Heil Hitler!"

holding their palms up flat. The Social Democrats were for
the Republic and carried its black, red and gold flag. They
each led frequent marches through the streets of Thalstadt,
singing with heavy men's voices and rending the air with
heavy-booted tread. Often they marched at night, carrying
torches; and long after they had disappeared along the
nighttime streets, a streak of fire like a comet's tail stained
the low edge of the sky and the wind was acrid as from a
distant conflagration.

"Heidelberg . . . Heigersdorf . . . Hildesheim. . . ."
The insistent radio voice droned on.

Eva drew the cover over her ears to shut out the sound.
But even with her eyes closed tight, the ghostly map of
Germany stood out against the dark—a playful puppy
pointed across the Polish Corridor to snap East Prussia up
between its open fangs, with the Lost Territories of the
Versailles Treaty shaded in neatly to the east and west,
exactly as on the map at school.

Of the grown-ups, only Grandfather had refused to stay
up beyond his usual bedtime hour. "The sleep before
midnight is the best," he had said. "The winning candidate
will make allowances in my case. We two old people need
our rest."

There had been a burst of laughter in the other room and
under it, no doubt, Grandfather had made his well-timed
exit, basking in their applause. Grown-up jokes did not
always make much sense, but even Eva got the point
for once: Grandfather had predicted the outcome of the
election! There was—or so it seemed to her sleep-
heavy ears—an undercurrent to the spurt of laughter in
the room next door: relief, perhaps, that old Field Mar-

shall von Hindenburg would be Reichspresident again; not
Hitler. Hitler was a queer little man with piercing eyes and
a rasping voice, who spoke in a queer kind of German about
taking back the territories lost after the war and about the
Shame of Versailles. Some people were afraid of him and
some made fun of him, but no one in the room next door
wanted him to be Reichspresident.

Now it was morning. Below her window, on the square,
the cobblestones glistened in the sunlight. There was still
the scent of rain, but also the scent of green and growing
things—the scent of Thalstadt on an April morning. It had
been a wet spring, this early spring of 1932, and yet a mild
and sunny one at times. "A harvest spring," Anna called it,
announcing that the cherries would be plumper and
sweeter this year than in many a season. Anna had grown
up in the orchard valley of the Rems and knew as much
about cherries as there was to know.

Anna opened the door abruptly and surveyed the room
with a frown. "No slippers on your feet," she said, making
it sound as irreparable as if she had said: No head on your
shoulders.

Groping for her missing slipper with one indifferent foot,
Eva considered asking Anna who had won the election, but
thought better of it. Anna, most probably, would neither
know nor care. "Politics is men's business," Eva had heard
her say more than once. "Where I come from, in the
Remstal," she would add primly, "women don't bother
about such things."

Perhaps Anna was right. Perhaps it was better to know
about rain and seasons and cherry trees than to know about
governments. Governments came and went in Germany;

even in Eva's young life, there had been so many. But April mornings in Thalstadt were always the same: clear and bright, full of unspoken promises. No matter who won elections in Berlin.

"Get washed and dressed quickly now," Anna muttered from the door. "Grandfather is waiting to have his breakfast served. Leave it to you to oversleep on a morning like this!"

It was only then that Eva remembered. She decided to wear her blue dress, even though it was a school day. Blue was Grandfather's favorite color, and this was Grandfather's day.

The door to her parents' room stood ajar. Her mother was already in the kitchen with Anna, but her father was shaving from the little porcelain mug on his dresser, his finely boned cheek and chin outlined under the thick foam as under a close-cropped white beard. He was listening to the radio on his night table, intent on the announcer's voice. When he became aware of Eva, his eyes smiled back at her in the mirror. Without his glasses, they were strikingly like her own: dark and grave, the high curve of the cheekbone lending them a subtly Oriental cast.

". . . his appreciation for the renewed confidence of the German people . . ." the radio voice was saying. If it meant that Hindenburg had been elected again, it did not seem to make her father noticeably happy.

In the dining room, Grandfather received Eva's birthday congratulations in dignified silence. She was glad they were alone at the table: formalities embarrassed her, and she had often seen Grandfather dispose of them with a shrug —though, at times, she rather suspected he secretly enjoyed them.

"Well, eighty years old, young lady," Grandfather

mused, smoothing his white mustaches. "How old, in fractions of a century, would you say that makes me?" Teasing her about arithmetic, her least favorite subject, had become as much a part of Grandfather's breakfasts with Eva as his morning coffee.

"Eight-tenths?" It had come too quickly to be the right answer.

"Let's call it four-fifths—it sounds younger," Grandfather said wryly. Old people had a way of being proud of their years, as if long life were a personal achievement rather than a mysterious gift. At the same time, one was expected to express surprise when they revealed their age.

Her mother, already in her sheer holiday blouse with the full long sleeves, hurried in with the breakfast tray. She picked up Grandfather's cup and filled it from the tall silver coffee urn reserved for special occasions.

"All my best wishes, Father! Jonas has gone for your morning paper. He'll join us presently."

Grandfather drummed his fingers on the tablecloth. "When one spends half the night talking . . ."

He let the sentence trail over their uneasy heads. Grandfather disapproved of his son's late hours. "Jonas comes to life only after midnight," he would say, hinting that the political discussions in the living room were robbing him of his own sleep next door. But though he considered his son the main offender, it was his son's *wife* to whom he always complained.

Anna brought in the coffee ring and wiped a sugar-spattered finger on her apron. "My congratulations, Herr Bentheim," she said formally, shaking Grandfather's hand.

"Thank you, Anna. I will never be too old to appreciate your excellent coffee!" And Grandfather raised his cup in a salute to her. Then he glanced at his pocket watch and resolutely snapped it shut. "I trust Jonas will forgive us if we begin."

The doorbell rang, stormily. Only Ella and Uschi would ring like that. Eva hastily sipped at her hot cocoa; it was past seven on the big clock above Roeblin's watch store across the street, and Ella disliked being kept waiting. There was, it seemed to Uschi and Eva, an almost endless number of things on Ella's list of dislikes, and experience had taught them to pay careful attention to every one of them.

"Congratulations, Grandfather!" her cousins cried, bursting through the door.

They ran to Grandfather's chair and threw their arms about him: Ella, tall for her thirteen years, her sweater a trifle snug across the front of her dress; Uschi, little and round, her bobbed hair curling disarmingly over her freckled forehead. Uschi hated her freckles; she was forever saving pennies for tiny tubes and jars of creams at the Crown Apothecary next door to Roeblin's, and once Eva had seen her sneak a dab of powder from Aunt Gustl's dressing table. But Uschi was foolish. The freckles were her only imperfection, and like a pinch of salt in a sweet dessert, they served to heighten her prettiness rather than detract from it. Everything about Uschi was small: her pouting mouth, her upturned nose, her well-formed ears. Everything except her eyes, which were wide and green like Hexle's, with a perpetually baffled look, beneath the sweep of long and enviably curled lashes. And yet it was Ella, with her darkly severe face and the slash of heavy eyebrows knotted in a permanent scowl, at whom people looked first, and longest.

"Eva is making us late for school, Aunt Martha," Ella promptly began, but let herself be pacified for the moment by a large helping of freshly baked coffee cake.

"I'll look out for the streetcar," she announced and took up her station at the window, glaring at the big clock between bites.

"Good morning, Jonas," Grandfather said archly as his son joined them at the table.

"And a good morning for two old gentlemen it is, indeed," Eva's father replied drily. He handed Grandfather the morning newspaper. "Your candidate was reelected. Congratulations, Father!"

"Thank you, Jonas—for me and my candidate," Grandfather said imperturbed, glancing at the picture of the aged Reichspresident with the martial mustaches. He narrowed his eyes at the print, not deigning to reach for his glasses. " *'Hindenburg Wiedererwaehlt!'* I could not have wished for a better birthday present than to see Hindenburg reelected."

His son shrugged. "The last best hope of the democratic coalition against Hitler—a tired old relic of the monarchy, a *Junker* general from the landed gentry. If he betrays the trust the Weimar parties placed in him, they will have no one to blame but themselves."

Grandfather reached for one of his finger-thin cigars. He cut off the tip with the tiny blunt-nosed scissors he always carried in his vest pocket and leaned back comfortably, watching the smoke curl over his empty cup. "I won't spend my eightieth birthday worrying about it, Jonas," he said, a faint flicker of irritation in his shrewd old eyes.

"There is the streetcar!" Ella called from the window.

The girls left hurriedly, clattering down the stairs and out into the wind-swept, sunlit square. They ran toward the streetcar, the warm breeze whipping their skirts about their legs. Running, Eva slipped off her coat; the sun had drained the air of the last memory of rain; it would be a lovely day.

2 ⚘⚘⚘

It was Grandfather's day.

From the door to the crowded living room, it seemed to Eva as if all the world—or half of Thalstadt, at least—had come to pay its respects to him this noon. His armchair was surrounded by well-wishers shaking his hand and drinking to his health; the din of voices was bewildering; and moving through the cigar smoke, flustered and smiling her weary hostess smile, Eva's mother passed trays of little frosted cakes to the ladies in the sofa corner.

Aunt Hanni, tiny on perilously high and pointed heels, her white hair artfully arranged for the occasion, was pouring liqueur into amber-tinted glasses. She was talking with Herr Valtary, a balding, suavely handsome man who had attended the Gymnasium with Eva's father and, having rediscovered him some years ago the owner of a bookstore, found him a ready customer for the art books he sold.

"Your brother's painting is being much admired," Aunt Hanni told Herr Valtary, waving her hand toward the open door to the drawing room, through which a steady stream of visitors was passing.

Herr Valtary clicked his heels and bowed from the waist.

During the war he had been a second lieutenant in the Kaiser's army, and remnants of past glories clung to him like shreds of the epaulets the revolutionaries had torn from the officers' shoulders. His brother—"a famous Munich artist," Ella had whispered importantly—had completed a portrait of Grandfather. It was a gift from the Bentheim family in honor of Grandfather's eightieth birthday and had arrived during the morning, while Eva was at school.

She caught a glimpse of Uschi's pink sash in the drawing room and slipped in after her. A half-circle of people, her father among them, had loosely formed itself before the far wall of the room. There, next to the somber painting of his long-dead wife, hung the new portrait of Grandfather. Grandfather, as she had seen him across the table on all the quiet mornings of her childhood: a small man, tidily put together, with cool eyes and a short white beard that came to a neatly trimmed point.

She stood and stared, spellbound. There was something about Grandfather's portrait that was more striking than mere physical likeness. Something that set it apart from the other pictures in the room: the pencil sketches of the slanting roofs and narrow streets of the Old City; the fluid pastels of ladies in floppy feather hats and flowing evening cloaks; the puzzling and intriguing shapes and textures that were called modern art.

"Alex Valtary, like all true artists, observes not only with his eyes," she had once heard her father say, and she had wondered what he meant. Suddenly she understood. For there, in the painting, somewhere beneath the cool composure of the eyes, was a giveaway tenderness, revealed for only a brief, unguarded moment for those who could see.

Behind her, something had changed. It had grown

utterly silent. Uschi, her face as pink as her sash, pointed toward the living room.

It was Ella. She stood at the window next to Grandfather's chair, the opened pages of the *Thalstadt Guardian* in her broad hands.

". . . 'one of its most highly regarded citizens and businessmen,'" she read out slowly, stumbling a little over the words. Behind her, watching her fondly with a proprietory smile on his owlish features, stood Uncle Ludwig.

"'We would indeed be remiss in our position as a spokesman for public opinion in Thalstadt,'" Ella went on, emboldened by the deferential silence around her and the comforting realization that she was nearing the bottom of the page, "'should we fail to extend our best neighborly wishes to Herr Jakob Bentheim for many more happy and prosperous years in our town.'" Ella folded the paper precisely and placed it on the table, next to the crystal bowl filled with birthday cards and telegrams.

There was a clearing of throats and a scraping of chairs, as if a performance had ended. The visitors were leaving; Grandfather's name in print conferred a subtly exalted status on all those present; whatever followed could hardly equal an editorial mention in the *Thalstadt Guardian*.

But in the suddenly empty hall, the front bell sounded once more. Anna appeared in the door and beckoned to Eva's mother. They conferred in whispers, her mother touching her fingers to her hair and glancing quickly about the room, as if to assure herself that the morning deluge of callers had left it presentable.

"*Der Herr Rabbiner*, Father," she told Grandfather with a little sigh, and hurried to the door.

The rabbi? Uschi and Eva could hardly believe their ears. It seemed an astonishing thing for the rabbi to do—to leave the hallowed aura of his habitat and come into the Bentheim living room! In the pulpit, Rabbi Gideon was a remote and solitary figure, taller by far, it seemed to Eva, than ordinary men who walked across doorsteps and paid calls on their neighbors. At the very least, one might have expected the distant echoes of organ tones to herald his arrival.

It was a disappointment, almost, to see the rabbi enter quite simply—and without having to incline his head.

"I am deeply honored, Herr Rabbiner," Grandfather said, rising for the first time and extending his hand. "You know my sons, of course—my widowed daughter, Frau Johanna Strauss, whose son is studying law at Heidelberg —my daughters-in-law—and our three young ladies."

Rabbi Gideon shook hands with everyone and sat down next to Grandfather.

"I am here not only for myself, Herr Bentheim, but also in the name of our congregation. My very best wishes! It is a pleasure to find you looking as youthful as ever."

He accepted a glass of wine from Eva's father and raised it in a toast. "*L'chayim*, Herr Bentheim—a long and healthy life! And may your house be blessed even as that other Jakob's house!"

"*L'chayim!*" Grandfather replied gravely, taking a small sip. "I've always known you to be a learned and pious man, Herr Rabbiner," he said, after a momentary pause during which he had sat and watched the smoke curl from his thin cigar, as if undecided whether to speak or not. "Your visit now proves that you are a magnanimous man as well. For

I'm afraid I am less than deserving of it," he finished with a faint smile.

The rabbi spread his pale hands. "You judge yourself too harshly, dear Herr Bentheim. I won't deny that all of us would like to enjoy your presence at the services more often. But to remember the widows and orphans, to walk in the paths of righteousness, is more pleasing to the All Highest than the most zealous attendance at His tabernacle. Of course," the rabbi added with a fine smile, "the best way is to combine the two!"

He leaned forward and placed his hand on the arm of Grandfather's chair. "But nothing can keep two Rhinelanders apart, can it? When I came to Thalstadt many years ago, fresh from the seminary, you showed your *Landsmann* many kindnesses. And I well remember your father, may he rest in peace, who was known throughout the Rhineland as a scholar and a saintly man."

"A scholar and a *Tzaddik*, yes," Grandfather replied thoughtfully, using the Hebrew word. "A good man, a devout Jew. And yet my mother, always poor, always harried and worn, died in her fortieth year, and my four brothers left for America to seek the future they could not hope to build for themselves in their native land."

He flicked the long ashes from his cigar with an air of finality. "I must have been quite young, Herr Rabbiner, when I decided the old ways, the ways of my father, could never be my own. I did not covet riches, but neither did I intend to have my wife and children suffer hardship and want. As for the rest, I content myself with burning a *Jahrzeit* candle each year in memory of my departed parents and my good wife, and rest secure that He to whom I owe a long and blessed life knows that it has also been a life for which I owe apologies to none."

Eva had rarely heard Grandfather speak so solemnly and at such length before; she wondered if his words, delivered with a calm incisiveness, had offended the rabbi.

But he said nothing to suggest they had. After a moment, he rose: tall and haggard in his dark suit, towering over Grandfather and yet somehow frailer, more vulnerable, than the older man. He shook Grandfather's hand and turned to leave, stepping aside at the door to let Anna carry in a great white-ribboned basket filled with red roses and carnations.

Grandfather opened the little white envelope curiously. " 'On the occasion of your eightieth birthday, a small token of neighborly esteem. S. Hallenbeck, Senior,' " he read aloud, unable to conceal a fleeting smile of satisfaction.

He turned to the rabbi. "From our friendly competitor and neighbor on the square," he explained, though an explanation was hardly necessary. Who in Thalstadt would fail to recognize the name of S. Hallenbeck, who owned the largest department store in town?

"Perhaps my way has not been without its measure of contribution, Herr Rabbiner. I won't deny that I prize my standing in the town community, and I like to think that, in its modest way, it has helped consolidate goodwill toward us all. We have come a long way, we Jews of Germany, since the times when my grandfather had to step down from the sidewalk at the demand of any passerby. This day has proved it to me once again—and nothing can turn the clock back anymore!"

The rabbi took his hand. "*Ihr Wort in Gottes Ohren*, Herr Bentheim," he said quietly. "Your word into the ears of God."

3 ✣✣✣

Grandfather's birthday dinner was to be held at the Rathskeller, the family had agreed. Herr Engelberth, the proprietor, would not have had it otherwise.

"The Rathskeller is a piece of Thalstadt, and so is Jakob Bentheim," he had declared, geniality flowing from his pink-cheeked smile. "They do honor unto each other, and that is as it should be."

For more years, almost, than could be counted, Grandfather had gone to the Rathskeller for his mid-morning jug of wine. Once, when Eva was very small, he had taken her along. She remembered the steep flight of stone steps and the cellar coolness and dimness below—a soothing dimness after the glare and hustle of the Marktplatz above. Copper gas lamps hung from the smoke-filmed beams of the arched ceiling; their flames threw flickering shadows against the paneled walls. The long oaken table at which Grandfather took his place was called the *Stammtisch*, and the elderly men on the wooden bench beside him were his *Stammtisch* brothers: Herr Roeblin, the watchmaker; Herr Pfaff, who owned the flower shop on Neckarstrasse; Herr Allmendinger, the notary; and Herr Kroner of the Crown

Apothecary. In the vaulted hall their voices had a hollow ring, and the sip of cool white wine Eva tasted from grandfather's tall, ornamented stein had a tart, tingling taste, like the taste of autumn. There was something solemn and austere about the Rathskeller, some quality reminiscent of the interior of the spired church where Anna went on Sunday mornings to kneel and pray. In the Rathskeller, the Deity was not God, but Custom and Changelessness. The very air seemed aged, as if it had been bottled and sealed and held in readiness for special occasions.

Herr Engelberth received the Bentheims at the cellar steps, his face rosier and more genial than ever under the neatly parted white hair.

He held Grandfather's hand as if it were something precious. "My very esteemed Herr Bentheim, allow me to congratulate you on this joyous occasion, both on behalf of myself and my establishment, which you have graced with your presence these many years."

He placed his arm about Grandfather's shoulder and led him to his seat at the head of the table, which today was covered with a gleaming white cloth and laden with flowers. Two rows of smiling faces turned toward them —familiar faces, for the most part, relatives, friends, and neighbors—but also others whom Eva recognized only by sight or not at all. She had never realized how many people Grandfather knew. Was that what growing old meant: adding other lives to one's own, along with the adding of the years?

"Hoch soll er leben, hoch soll er leben, dreimal hoch!" sang the

members of the *Stammtisch* with rusty old men's voices, raising their well-filled steins.

Watchmaker Roeblin, the youngest and nimblest of them, rose from his seat and delicately eased his paunch over the edge of the table. "Since Jakob Bentheim is not a man of many words, I shall not tax his patience with my oratory. Suffice it to say, after some thirty-odd years, most of us here at the *Stammtisch* have become used to his whims and pecularities. We're even willing to put up with them until his *one hundredth* anniversary, which, judging from his predilection for the Rathskeller wine, he shows every intention of reaching!"

A smile brushed the corners of Grandfather's mouth. He tugged at his trim mustache and raised his hand to quiet the applause. "If my neighbor Rudi Roeblin were to pay more attention to the clock outside his store, instead of thinking up speeches to insult me, perhaps my granddaughters might manage to get to school on time!"

In the ensuing laughter, there was a momentary turning of amused faces in the direction of the girls; then all eyes were once more centered on Herr Roeblin. He had taken something from the pocket of his coat and placed it, not without some show of ceremony, on Grandfather's folded napkin. A small white box with the inscription, ROEBLIN'S HOUSE OF CLOCKS embossed in glossy gold, and under it, in finer, fainter print: *Where Time Never Stands Still.*

"We knew you wouldn't part with your favorite old watch, Bentheim," Herr Roeblin said huskily. "So we decided to surprise you with the next best thing—a new watch chain. And since that dependable old watch of yours was purchased by your good wife a great many years ago at none other than Rudi Roeblin's, those present are invited to judge for themselves the accuracy of Roeblin's clocks and watches—including the one outside my store!"

This time, even Grandfather was left speechless. All he could do was hold up the little white box and let the golden chain inside gleam in the light of the copper lanterns, for all to see.

Then the door to the Rathskeller kitchen flung open and the waiters, under the vigilant eye of Herr Engelberth, carried the steaming trays to the tables.

Later, after the guests had left, the tavern owner followed the Bentheims to the top of the Rathskeller steps and stood, pink and genial with his hands extended, under the striped awning above his door.

"You have surpassed your reputation as a gracious host, Herr Engelberth," Eva's father said, in the light tone reserved for occasions of some moment.

"It is always a pleasure to play host to the Bentheim family," the tavern owner replied. Then he added, good-humoredly, "May I make reservations now for your Herr Father's *next* big anniversary, five years from now?"

The grown-ups laughed, a trifle wearily; it had been a long day. Only Eva's father seemed about to reply to Herr Engelberth's jesting proposal, peering into the other's face intently, almost probingly. But after a moment, he turned and followed the others through the late April light, without looking back.

The square was busy at this hour. At the newspaper kiosk on the corner, men were already taking down election posters and pasting on new ones: HINDENBURG WIEDERERWAEHLT!—Hindenburg reelected! With sweeping strokes of their dripping brushes, they slapped on a photo of the aged president in his old uniform and pointed Prussian helmet, looking grim and battle-proven next to a poster announcing an emergency meeting of the Thalstadt NSDAP—the party of Hitler.

Grandfather lightly struck the kiosk with his cane, just below Hindenburg's row of metals. "*He'll* show them who is master in the house!" he said, and yawned unashamedly. It had been a long day.

4 ⚘⚘⚘

Frau Ackermann always began the school day with a song. Her rich, mellow alto flowed like the calm current of a river, on which their thin, high voices rose to the surface in spurts and ripples. When the ripples had swelled into a torrent, Frau Ackermann held out her large, sun-tanned hand firmly, soothingly, and laid her head to one side as if she were listening to something far away.

Her hand waved them to their seats.

"In order to sing with feeling and expression, class, it is not necessary to shout at the top of one's voice," she said drily, and turned to the blackboard.

May 27, 1932, she wrote under a fine spray of chalk. *German dictation.*

"Many songs popularly regarded as folksongs are actually poems by the great poets of Germany, set to music by her renowned composers," she began to dictate slowly, leaving her desk to keep a close watch on half-turned heads and straying eyes.

It was not easy to put one's mind on dictation with the May breeze drifting into the classroom and the trees in the schoolyard bright with new leaves. Reluctantly, Eva turned her eyes from the window and bent her head over her notebook. Frau Ackermann, walking between the rows of benches with her lithe, springy step (like a tigress ready to pounce, Diete Goetz had once muttered), gave her a quick nod. If one had to be in school at all on a morning like this, it helped having a teacher like Frau Ackermann. She might know when one failed to pay full attention, but she would never be *really* angry as long as one honestly tried.

It was one of the good things about Frau Ackermann that Ella and Uschi had told her in advance. "Frau Ackermann isn't like any other teacher," they had said. "She is *just*, absolutely just!" Everyone knew that Frau Bleile, the third-grade teacher, had favorites, and Fräulein Fink, in fourth, held grudges. One did one's utmost to pass through the purgatory of the fourth-grade examinations into the paradise of the upper school, *Realklasse* 1, where Frau Ackermann reigned supreme and dispensed stern but incontestable justice. Frau Ackermann had become a legend in Buchberg School, but unlike most legends, she was entirely true.

There were other things about Frau Ackermann, too —things that Ella and Uschi had failed to mention. Her hair, except for a few faded strains, was exactly the color of the glossy chestnuts she placed on their desks for nature study. The generous white-toothed smile with which she rewarded a clever answer or even an exceptionally probing question gave her a faintly predatory look. Her rare but terrible fits of anger made them huddle behind their desk tops, seeking futile shelter from the downpour of her wrath, and left them spent, but somehow cleansed and renewed, ready to bask once more in the all-redeeming benevolence of her smile.

The teacher had returned to her desk. "Can anyone give an example to illustrate our lesson of today?" She leafed through the little book in which she entered their grades. "Monika von Ahlem?"

There was not the slightest evidence to suspect that Monika was Frau Ackermann's favorite. Frau Ackermann *had* no favorites. If she called on Monika perhaps a little more often than she called on anyone else, if she smiled the least bit more brightly while addressing her, it must have been for the sheer pleasure of pronouncing so lofty and melodious a name, a titled name with an old and romantic ring even in these prosaic republican times.

Monika rose with that air of lassitude on her elegant face that Diete Goetz (who called it a pinched little spinster's face) ascribed to a tired line of titled ancestors. The song "Das Heidenröslein," Monika said without hesitation, was actually a poem written by Johann Wolfgang von Goethe, and set to music. "There are three versions," she added, shrugging her pale hair back over her shoulder, "including the one by Schubert."

"An excellent application of the lesson, Monika," Frau Ackermann said, turning from her book to acknowledge other hands raised for recognition.

Eva was holding her hand up, too, holding it carefully steady because Frau Ackermann had said that it was "undisciplined" to wave one's hand excitedly in class. She was going to say, "The Lorelei"—a song she had often sung with her mother and then discovered in her new schoolbook, *A Sheaf of German Poems*. But just then Dorle Hohnegger caught Frau Ackermann's eye and called out, " 'The Lorelei!' By Heinrich Heine!"

" 'The Lorelei,' yes—a great German poem," Frau

Ackermann said. "A poem from the wellsprings of the German soul—no wonder it is often mistakenly thought to be a folksong, rather than the creation of a great German poet." And she gave Dorle one of her most benevolent smiles.

Did Frau Ackermann know that Heine had been Jewish? Eva wondered. One of Germany's stepsons, her father had called him—"never fully accepted, often attacked and defamed, in his lifetime and since. A poet and a brilliant critic of his time—born a century too soon."

Heine had died in Paris—"in exile," her father had said—homesick for the Germany that rejected its "greatest lyric poet next to Goethe," as the note in *A Sheaf of German Poems* described him. Did Frau Ackermann know? Eva wondered.

Renate Reinhardt tugged at Eva's sleeve and pointed across the aisle toward the boys' rows. There, just ahead of them, Horst Reuter sat hunched over his desk, his penholder furtively poised between his fingers. Shielded by Anton Huber's back, he stealthily thrust the sharp point of his pen into a threadbare spot on Anton's neatly pressed shirt. For once, even Frau Ackermann's keen eyes failed to take notice; there was no way of stopping Horst without committing the unthinkable: a breach of the class code against tattling. Only Klaus Herzog could save Anton now—Klaus who had seen and who sat near enough to Anton to give him silent warning. Renate and Eva signaled frantically, but Klaus had already turned away, his face blank. In *Realklasse* 1 of Buchberg School, the children always looked away when Horst played one of his tricks.

Horst's pen caught a worn thread in Anton's shirt. A flush of triumph spread slowly over Horst's face, the kind of look Eva had seen come over him on the ball field when one of his glancing shots struck down an obstinate opponent. Horst's hard shots always swung the game for his team; his feats of hitting and dodging at *Völkerball* had won him the awed allegiance of the class. The boys submitted humbly to his heavy-handed sway; if there were occasional faint rumblings of rebellion, the guilty were swiftly unmasked, isolated, and punished, long before the scattered subterranean revolt could burst into fullblown insurrection.

As for the girls, they bore his insults with astonishing complacency; indeed, they bore them proudly, like badges of honor. With perfect impunity, Horst was permitted to waddle about the schoolyard like a duck, in spiteful parody of Inge Beisswanger's walk, or mock with gross exaggeration the singsong Saxon accent of little Helga Boehm —affronts that would have resulted in tears and furious protests had they been committed by anyone else.

Their attitude puzzled Eva; and, try as she might, she was unable to share it.

Once, during recess, Horst had brushed past her in the hall and quickly pinned her arm behind her shoulder. And when she twisted and fought, more outraged at the enforced closeness of his body than at the sudden searing jolt of pain, his lazily handsome mouth had formed the whispered words, "Little Jap!"

She drew back, stunned; what he had said was not at all the same as when her cousin, Stefan, teasingly called her Madame Butterfly.

Horst dropped his hand abruptly: Frau Ackermann was calling Anton Huber's name! Jumping to his feet, Anton suggested "The Good Comrade," a breezy marching song that was a favorite when class R. I. went on one of its outings. "The words are by Ludwig Uhland, 1787–1862," Anton added, his eyes carefully averted from Frau Ackermann's black book of grades. Marks meant a great deal to Anton; he was a scholarship student who had come to Buchberg School only the month before from the free *Volksschule*. Anton wanted to become an engineer, he had confided to Eva and Renate, and invent new machines that would make work safer and cleaner for the men in the factories. Anton's father built automobiles at the great Dietz works on the Neckar River, he had added, almost as if he felt called upon to explain the ambitiousness of his goal.

"Splendid, Anton!" Frau Ackermann's smile radiated encouragement. "One of our own Swabian poets, Uhland! Perhaps you will come up to the blackboard and write down some of the titles that have been suggested, so we may enter them in our notebooks."

But before Anton could step away from his desk, Horst's hand lunged forward once more, and with an upward thrust of his pen he finished what he had started. Between two rows of curious, weighing eyes, Anton walked up to the blackboard, unaware that his shirt was nearly ripped in two. He picked up the chalk, standing on tiptoes to write the first line, then paused uneasily, flustered by the subdued whisper behind his back.

A pall had fallen over the classroom. But suddenly, as if at the secret bidding of Horst's narrowed eyes, a ripple of laughter rose to the surface, a forced and feeble sound but with an edge of bravado; for it was easier to laugh on Horst's side than to keep silent with those he taunted. At the blackboard, Anton stood twisting the chalk between his fingers, his thin face beseechingly turned toward the teacher, his eyes bewildered, at bay.

Frau Ackermann, aware of what had happened with one swift, wrathful glance, braced her tanned hands against the swelling tide of laughter as if she were damming a dyke. "There are three things I will not abide," she said softly, but with an ominous flashing of her eyes. "What are they, class?"

The laughter spurted and ceased. They sat and looked at one another sheepishly, suddenly sobered, chastened. A power higher even than Horst had taken command in the classroom; as if by some compelling touch of grace, the forces of darkness receded before the forces of light.

"Lying, cheating, and hurting someone's feelings," they replied in hollow chorus. All of them: those who had giggled and those who had not, even those who had often themselves been wronged—as if by their blind adulation of Horst, by their mute acquiescence in his hurtful deeds, they had themselves been tainted with his guilt.

Frau Ackermann nodded her curt nod of satisfaction. "And you, Horst Reuter? What have you to say for yourself?"

Horst stared at his notebook, his face flushed, but his fingers still clasped tightly about the offending pen. "It was just an old shirt," he said sullenly. "My father will pay him for another one."

Frau Ackermann clenched her hands as if she were bridling her runaway anger only at a supreme effort of her will. "Will he, indeed, Horst? And do you really think you can pay Anton in money for the loss of his shirt? Perhaps the old shirt suited him fine, as only the old and long-accustomed has a way of doing. Such things can never be restored by money, Horst. Nor can you pay Anton for the hurt and humiliation you have made him endure."

The teacher paused. Gently, she took the chalk from Anton's hand and led him back to his seat.

"I shall not have you ask Anton's forgiveness, Horst," she said tiredly above the ringing of the bell. "There are things for which forgiveness must be earned."

5 ❦❦❦

Stefan was back!

One afternoon as Eva was coming home from school, there he was on the sidewalk outside their door. He wore a bright new ribbon on his student's cap and two new fencing scars on his smooth cheek and chin. He gave her a quick hug and tousled her hair, expertly tilting his cigarette between two outstretched fingers. Stefan always gave her a hug when he came home from Heidelberg, but on this day she felt a new awareness of his touch, as if it were happening for the first time. Perhaps she had never quite seen before how nice Stefan looked, because he wore horn-rimmed glasses and was her cousin.

"How tall you've grown, Madame Butterfly," Stefan said perfunctorily. It was the sort of thing grown-ups were always saying to children.

He flipped his cigarette into the gutter. Squatting on his heels, he tinkered with the front wheel of his motorcycle, whistling softly off-key. Stefan loved Brahms, especially his violin concerto. But because Stefan shared the family affliction of the Bentheims, tone deafness, he could remember only a few bars. These he whistled interminably and badly—to buoy up his spirits, to express satisfaction, or for no discernible reason at all. Sometimes, when he was gone for months at a time and his features grew vague in Eva's memory, she merely needed to conjure up the shrill pitch of his whistling, and Stefan's face would begin to form itself about it: his mobile mouth and the clear gray eyes with their slight squint of cultivated disdain.

Stefan stretched his legs and wiped his grease-stained fingers on his handkerchief. "Almost as good as new!" He gave the shining fender an affectionate pat and pushed his cap over his forehead at a jaunty angle. "Can't allow old Rocinante to run down, you know. What would Heidelberg be without him?"

Eva laughed. Stefan's motorcycle didn't look a bit like Don Quixote's bony old horse.

"Do you use your motorcycle for study trips, Stefan?" she inquired. Frau Ackermann frequently took her class on tours of historic places: the Grave Chapel on the Rotenberg, with its great vaults and royal sarcophagi; or to Schloss Solitude, the "Swabian Sans Souci" with the famous desk of Karl Der Dicke that was ingeniously hollowed out to allow for the regal girth of its late owner.

For some unexplained reason, Stefan laughed uproariously. "You go tell Grandfather about my study trips, Butterfly. Grandfather doesn't appreciate my motorcycle."

Stefan creased his face into sardonic lines and rubbed his chin, stroking a short, invisible beard. "I am paying your tuition, my boy, to afford you an education, not to have you gallivant about the Heidelberg countryside."

They both burst out laughing. Grandfather himself could hardly have kept from laughing, had he seen and heard how perfectly Stefan mimicked him! There was only one thing: though it was true that Grandfather *might* have said these very words in just this very way, Eva had never heard him say them. She doubted that Stefan had either.

Her mother was coming from the market, carrying a basket of peaches in one hand and a mesh shopping bag filled with greens in the other.

Stefan rushed to open the door for her. "Allow me, fairest of women . . ." He covered his chest with his ribboned cap and made an exaggerated bow.

Her mother laughed, flustered but not displeased. The pastel flowers of her dress under the wide-brimmed straw hat made her face look soft and young. And yet it seemed to Eva that the words had slipped from Stefan's lips too glibly, merely because one was expected to compliment ladies, just as one was supposed to tell children they had grown tall. Words came easily to Stefan, but sometimes now there seemed to be a wrong note in what he was saying, as if here, too, he was missing the key.

"Will you join us for supper, Stefan?" her mother asked on the stairs.

"Delighted," Stefan shot back, and gallantly carried the basket of peaches the rest of the way.

Passing up dessert, Stefan wondered if he might have cognac with his coffee.

"One of the small amenities of home," he said ruefully, "after the rigors of university life."

Grandfather eased himself into his deep, sagging chair. He took a finger-thin cigar from his wooden cigar box and clipped off the tip with his vest-pocket scissors. "And what have you to say for your professors this semester, Stefan?"

"My professors?" Stefan asked innocently as he set down his glass. "Well, Grandfather, the professors are as they have always been—a bit more so, perhaps. The nationalists are dull lecturers but easy to please; the tide is going their way! The liberals talk brilliant balderdash, trying to mold us in the image of a new *Sturm und Drang* generation, drawing its sword to save the Holy Republic. They speak to us of Universal Peace and Solidarity with the Exploited Masses. But they have little sympathy to spare for their students and do their best to flunk a few pampered sons of the bourgeoisie while they still have the chance."

"With Heidelberg full of nationalists," Eva's father said mildly, "Stefan seems to have drawn all the liberals this year."

Stefan bit his lip. He had taken off his horn-rimmed glasses and looked to Eva like a bright and wicked little boy, not very different from the small sailor in his mother's satin-bound photo album.

"I see Mother's been telling tales out of school. I hope she hasn't painted too gloomy a picture for you, Uncle Jonas. Actually, I'm having trouble with only two courses, and in both—"

"—the blame is Professor Vollmar's, no doubt. A former delegate to the League of Nations in Geneva. One whose concern for peace and social justice you find so irresistibly amusing."

Stefan blushed, the fencing scars turning crimson on his cheek. "Dr. Vollmar is a fine old man, Uncle Jonas, and I respect him. But it's no secret at the university that he is opposed to the student fraternities and anyone connected with them. He's openly denounced them in the lecture hall—I'll admit that takes courage—calling them antidemocratic and ultranationalistic."

"Has he, Stefan? A year ago you might not have disagreed with him on this issue. But perhaps fraternity restrictions can be viewed with greater magnamity from the inside than from the ranks of the excluded."

"It's simply a matter of selectivity," Stefan objected somewhat lamely. "They can't let just anyone join. There are certain standards, qualifications—"

"Such as the proper name and religion, Stefan?"

"Fortunately for me," Stefan said with a disarming grin, "my father left me, if little else, a name that's conveniently neutral, shall we say? There have been Strausses on both sides of the dividing line—Gentiles as well as Jews." He shrugged. "And since I hold with Nietzsche that God is dead, I frankly see no point in listing a religious affiliation."

His uncle looked at him curiously. "You oversimplify, Stefan. Nietzsche may have succeeded in negating God, but no one, on either side of the 'dividing line,' as you call it, has yet succeeded in negating those who first experienced Him—perhaps *created* Him, if you prefer. You are who you are, Stefan; the sooner you discover who, the sooner you can be what you wish to be."

"Well, I have *made* some discoveries!" Stefan said with an air of mystery. "A trip to Worms with a new friend and mentor has finally opened fraternity doors to me!"

A trip to Worms! So Stefan's motorcycle had been put to good use, after all! In some as yet unexplained way, Eva understood, it had helped him attain the one thing on which he had set his heart. Now Grandfather would surely let him keep it.

Stefan twirled his cap, prolonging the suspense. "You see, I had to go to Worms to prove to myself what I have always felt to be true but could never substantiate, simply because no one before me had ever cared enough to find out. The Rathaus archives at Worms trace our family back over *centuries* in the Rhineland!"

Grandfather shrugged. "Hundreds of our families must have like histories, Stefan. The Jews came with the Romans. When the Crusaders saved us from hellfire by burning us in our synagogues, or baptized us by force beneath the waters of the Rhine, we had already lived our separate ways among them for generations."

"But can't you see what it all *means!*" Stefan said impatiently. "We Bentheims have lived on German soil far longer than those 'acceptable' Germans descended from the Slavs of Prussia or the Huguenot émigrés! As long, perhaps, as many of the proud families whose sons are pledged into the fraternities as a matter of course!"

"And on the basis of these 'extenuating circumstances,'" his uncle concluded wryly, "it was decided to close an eye in your case and let you join."

Stefan nodded. "Provisionally, backed by Heinz-Dietrich Hohnold's mentorship. To become final upon conclusive proof of merit—my duelling skills, compatibility with the fraternity's philosophy, its *Weltanschauung*. What it comes down to, I suppose, is making clear that one thinks and feels as a true German—a simple matter of demonstrating one's patriotism."

"What patriotism, Stefan? The kind that wallows in beer and wild-eyed speeches while cupboards are bare and children cannot go to school for lack of shoes? The patriotism that fans the ancient hatreds against France, subverts the Weimar Constitution, and waves the flag for yet another war? There is another patriotism, Stefan, one that might say today what Heine said a hundred years ago to the sham patriots of his own day: 'Plant the black, red and gold flag on the heights of German thought, make it the standard of free humanity, and I will shed my heart's blood for it!' "

Eva watched her father push back his cup and leave the table abruptly. Her mother gave him an anxious glance; Grandfather drummed his fingers on the arm of his chair, his face blank, his eyes haughtily half shut. Stefan twirled his cap, his lips pursed as if he were trying to drown out the other voice by silently whistling to himself. When he realized that the words had ceased to come, he looked up and absently patted his shirt pocket. His uncle noticed and offered him his cigarette case; their eyes met, and suddenly Stefan's lips curved into a smile.

"Your old professor could not have said it better, Uncle Jonas! You were Vollmar's student, weren't you, at Munich before the war? In those days there was still a point in quoting Heine—or Lessing or Goethe, for that matter. Today there is only Nietzsche—or Marx!"

"There is still right and wrong, Stefan. Good and evil. Those who defend the Republic and those who seek to destroy it."

"If it can be destroyed so easily, perhaps it deserves to be!" Stefan shouted, thumping the table with his fist. His cap dropped to the floor and lay there ignominiously, sharing Stefan's certain fall from grace. Eva stared at it aghast, not daring to restore it to its former splendor. She had never known anyone to talk back to her father in this

rude fashion; though others in the family might disagree
with him, they always did so respectfully. Stefan himself
must have become frightened by his own temerity; his face
went a shade redder and suddenly turned quite pale.

He leaned across the table, tilting his cigarette absently
between unsteady fingers. "Even if I agreed with your
judgment of the fraternities, Uncle, I would still join them
as an act of self-preservation. Germany is moving to the
Right. I support the nationalists because they are the last
bulwark against the Nazis!"

His uncle picked up Stefan's cap and brushed a grain of
dust from the bright band.

"If the Republic falls, Stefan," he said quietly, "your
scars and ribbons won't buy you entry into the Valhalla of
the new Reich."

Grandfather coughed his dry, old man's cough. He
raised himself from his deep chair and with surprising
agility switched on the reading light. Dusk had fallen over
the square, and the room had grown nearly dark; but it had
come about so slowly, so stealthily, that they had scarcely
been aware of it. Eva's mother, taking Grandfather's
gesture as a reprimand, hurried to light the ceiling lamp. Its
sudden brightness threw everything into sharp relief: the
pictures on the wall, the gleam of the old chest, the barefoot
Dresden goose girl and her flock behind the glass. It was
evening, and the city air was tinged with the first scents of
Thalstadt summers.

Grandfather took a peach from the fruit bowl and tested
its downy skin in his fine old hand. "I'm rather sorry your
uncle permitted you to turn this conversation into a debate
on politics and philosophy, Stefan. For my part, I am not

terribly concerned with your opinions on theology, fraternities, or Berlin politicians. What does interest me is your attendance at lectures, your devotion to your studies, and the quality of your academic work. I would advise you most urgently to improve on these, young man, or you may find me as lacking in sympathy as you repute your professors to be."

"*Jawohl*, Grandfather," Stefan said contritely, hanging his head. Then, as if he suddenly remembered something, he threw back his shoulders and firmly gripped Grandfather's hand. "Upon my word of honor as a German student," he said smartly, clicking his heels and bowing stiffly from the waist.

Soon after, while Eva was beginning her homework in her room, she heard the familiar clatter of Stefan's motorcycle outside and got to the window just as he roared down the *Gässle* and went out of sight. She stared after him moodily. She had been so glad to see Stefan again, to have him stay for supper, but somehow the evening had gone wrong from the start. Stefan's big words still whirled in her head: nationalists, last bulwark against the Nazis—and her father's grave voice in reply, "If the Republic falls, Stefan . . ."

She swallowed hard. Why did her father always have to bring in politics? What difference did it make what Stefan thought and did in Heidelberg? All Stefan really wanted was to be like everyone else and to go places on his motorcycle. Couldn't her father see that? She tried to be angry at her father for once, but it was no use: she knew

Stefan had changed, or the world outside had *made* him change, just as so many other things seemed to be changing. It was all part of "the times," she thought miserably, wondering if things would ever again be the way they used to be.

6 ✼✼✼

Twice a week, the day would begin with the arrival of Fräulein Brenner, the hairdresser. The bell would ring, shrilly and peremptorily (sounding very much the way Fräulein Brenner *looked*, with her sharp nose and piercing eyes), followed by Anna's footsteps in the hall and her grudging "Good morning" in response to the hairdresser's strenuously cheerful one.

"Ah, it is you, my dear Fräulein," Eva's mother called from the door to her room on this particular morning in July. "Do hurry in out of the weather!"

Fräulein Brenner set down her case and slipped off her raincoat, dripping water on Anna's newly waxed floor. "Fine day, Frau Bentheim. A bit of summer rain, fresh and cool—it smells so good!" Her sharp nose quivered with pleasure.

Fräulein Brenner had recently married, after a long and intermittent courtship whose peaks and pitfalls were faithfully shared with Eva's mother and, presumably, with a wide circle of other ladies. Strictly speaking, Fräulein Brenner was now Frau Schiller, but with a fine touch of professionalism she had retained her former name. Eva received this announcement with relief and a genuine feeling of respect: obviously, Fräulein Brenner had been aware that there was something faintly sacrilegious in taking a poet's name for the business of curling hair. Though all she would say about the matter was that "men come and go, Frau Bentheim, but one's good name is something to hold on to."

In her mother's room, the small spirit burner was already aglow, and a subtly medicinal whiff of smoke lingered incenselike in the air. Fräulein Brenner rustled into her starched coat and clicked her tongs over the low blue flame.

"Your hair is *dry!*" she told her client chidingly.

Eva's mother slipped out her comb and loosened her hair. It was an unassuming brown, already flecked lightly with gray, and thin and fine as a baby's. To Eva it was lovely hair, in a soft, vulnerable way like the coat of a bird. But her mother despaired of it and longed for the dark, abundant tresses of her sisters. For whatever confidence she could summon in facing her day, she considered herself beholden to Fräulein Brenner. And though she was usually so artless and innocent in her dealings with others, she was not above a bit of shameless flattery to keep the fickle favors of the hairdresser. Eva knew this and wondered, uneasily, if the Fräulein knew it too.

"How good of you to come so early this morning," her mother said, careful to keep her chin on her chest. "We'll be leaving for Ettingen in an hour, where Eva will spend part of her summer vacation with my parents. I don't know how I would have managed without you!"

"I wouldn't have done it for just anyone, Frau Bentheim," Fräulein Brenner said frostily. "I had to squeeze you in between Frau Dr. Kapf and Fräulein Appenzeller—she *dyes*, you know!" The latter was said in a stage whisper behind the back of the hairdresser's bony hand.

"Did you have time for breakfast?" Eva's mother asked.

"Please keep your head down, Frau Bentheim," Fräulein Brenner said tersely, testing the heat of the irons with a moistened forefinger. There was a faint hiss of steam. "Yes, I had Georg throw some eggs into the frying pan. Just because a man is out of work, I don't believe in him lying around in bed when the sun is up, do you, Frau Bentheim?"

"*Ach*," Eva's mother said, soothingly and inconclusively, declining to be drawn into a possible marital argument between the newlyweds.

Eva peeked through the curtains. Rain spattered drearily against the blurred windowpane. "But the sun hasn't come out yet, Fräulein Brenner," she pointed out politely.

"Eva!" her mother interrupted from somewhere beneath the flurry of activity around her bowed head. "I beg you, dear Fräulein, what makes children so forward nowadays? Would *we* have dreamed of breaking into adult conversation? In *our* youth?"

Fräulein Brenner brightened perceptibly. She was easily a dozen years older than Eva's mother. "Children are children, Frau Bentheim," she said magnanimously.

The tongs clicked above the murmur of their voices. Below Eva's window a truck unloaded its supplies at the back door of Grandfather's store; the shower had run its course. A man in a dark raincoat, collar upturned and hat tilted foppishly over his forehead, stood leaning against the wall of the Muenzer house across the street, impatiently tapping his foot. He took a last drag from his cigarette, flipped it into a puddle, and glanced up at their windows. Something about the briefly glimpsed face, shadowed by a stubble of beard, seemed familiar to Eva, though she felt certain that she had never met the man. She turned away with a shrug and opened the window to let in the clean-washed air, smelling of summer, of vacation days. It was time to leave for Ettingen; her mother was taking Fräulein Brenner to the door and calling to Eva from the hallway to get ready.

Leaning over the wet windowsill to retrieve a windblown corner of the gauzy curtain, Eva saw Fräulein Brenner with her magic carrying case coming out the front door. She crossed the street swiftly, her spindly heels clicking a staccato against the cobblestones. With a start of recognition, she saw the man in the raincoat and passed him with an angry toss of her head. But he had already caught up with her and roughly seized her arm. They stood stiffly, glaring at one another, his hand tightening about her arm. At last, Fräulein Brenner nodded warily, opened her navy blue pocketbook, and pushed a folded bill into his coat pocket. He let go of her at once and walked down the *Gässle* without looking back. The Fräulein turned also and continued toward the streetcar stop, rubbing her arm and walking shakily on her stiletto heels.

Poor Fräulein Brenner. Eva remembered the morning when she had first told them about her fiancé and had opened up that same navy blue pocketbook to show off a snapshot of herself with Georg, taken in one of those new automatic photo booths. His face had been clean-shaven then, his hair slicked back and minus the tilted hat, and his arm placed lightly and chivalrously about Fräulein Brenner's thin shoulder. But even then, Eva suddenly realized, there had been something furtive about that smooth and smiling face that had made her feel queasy. Poor Fräulein Brenner.

7 ⁂

On the way to the train station, setting out on a journey, Thalstadt always looked different from ordinary days. The streetcars and shops on the Königstrasse, the green sweep of lawns on the Schlossplatz, the shallow steps leading to the station tower—all carried a sharper imprint, a keener message to her leave-taking eyes. A scent of cinder and expectancy hung over the waiting rooms, and the omniscient voice of the stationmaster boomed over the bustling lobby: "Train to Karlsruhe, Heidelberg, Darmstadt —platform 5 . . . train to Schwaebisch Hall, Ansbach, Nuernberg—leaving now. . . ."

At last it was time for the train to Ettingen. Her father chose a smoker's compartment, and having placed their luggage and umbrellas in the rack overhead, at once opened his newspaper and lit a cigarette. Her mother folded a gauzy scarf over the soft waves that had emerged only shortly before from the clicking tongs and deft, bony fingers of Fräulein Brenner. Outside, on the dusky platform, a blond cosmetics vendor in a tight-fitting white skirt and blouse wheeled her cart down the long row of cars, chanting in rhythmic monotone: "Cologne, face cream, powder, soap. . . ." A few tardy travelers hurried toward the waiting train; others leaned over the lowered windows for a last handshake or an awkward embrace. Then the locomotive released its steam with a hiss and an ear-piercing whistle. The train shuddered and moved, gathered speed and rushed from the station. Soon the city streets were behind them, the suburban gardens with their bright splashes of russets and golds, the belt of freight yards and factories surrounding the town.

"There is the tunnel, Eva," her father said and pulled the window shut.

Darkness crashed over the train. Only the red ashes on her father's cigarette glowed reassuringly.

Then the train burst into the sunlight, into the rolling grassland of the Neckar banks. The wide river glistened in the haze. Peasant children stood below railroad trestles, gaping at the locomotive and waving their hands. Cows flicked their stringy tails, and pigs rolled unabashedly in the farmyard mud. From her seat at the window, Eva waved back at the reeling, beneficent world. "When angels travel, heaven smiles," Aunt Gustl had said, with heavy irony, seeing them off at their front door under an overhung, threatening sky. It must be a Bavarian saying, Eva thought, for no one else in Thalstadt ever said it. Leaning her face against the soot-streaked window splashed with sun, Eva noted, not without guilty satisfaction, that on the train to Ettingen the skies nearly always turned out to be fair, while on the rare occasions when the Upstairs traveled to Nuremberg, the weather was usually awful.

At the rural stations, country people got on the train, carrying baskets or bulky traveling cases long out of fashion. They scanned their city faces with circumspect curiosity, reserving judgment. Some, after a tentative remark on the weather, inquired about one's destination or made some passing, disapproving comment on the news of the day—"six million unemployed . . . Where does this leave the farmer?"—to which her father responded in his courteous, guarded way and with a rustle of paper and a flick of his slender wrist retreated behind the barrier of his newspaper. Meanwhile, everyone in the compartment unwrapped substantial wurst sandwiches or ate a hard-boiled egg with salt and buttered bread. Eating seemed to belong with railroad rides, even when the train was to take one no further than the next stop along the line.

For the Bentheims, the end of the journey came all too soon. As the train slowed to a halt on the familiar Ettingen platform, Eva's grandfather swung hastily through the station gate. He took off his hat and mopped his gloomy, loose-cheeked face with his great checkered handkerchief. His baggy trousers fluttered in the breeze. His jacket hung limply from his stooped, wide shoulders. Grandfather Weil was as big, ungainly, and irascible as Grandfather Bentheim was small, fastidious, and self-possessed.

Her grandparents' house, too, was altogether different from their own in Thalstadt. At home, there was a settled, final feeling about the rooms. The old Persian rugs and runners softened outlines and muffled sound. In Ettingen, dimensions were larger—or perhaps they only seemed so because the rooms were sparsely furnished and the oaken floors were bare. Steps echoed and voices rang in the cool, dark hall. A dry, minted scent hung over the house, like the scent of linen fresh off the clothesline on a windblown day.

The countryside, where Eva's grandparents had been raised, was never far from Ettingen, and nowhere nearer than in these vast and sober rooms.

Only the little white room at the end of the hall defied the austere quality of the old house. This was the domain of Sabine, her mother's youngest sister—as unmistakably Sabine's as the scoured, green-shaded kitchen was Grandmother's, as fascinating and unpredictable as were Sabine's own capricious moods. On the white-painted dresser, the sleek sculpted head of an ancient Egyptian queen kept its haughty distance from a flask of French perfume—both tantalizingly off-limits to Eva's hands under pain of Sabine's most serious displeasure. On the bookshelf, a linen-bound edition of Rilke lay in preposterous proximity to a music sheet of the latest hit song, and on the white-washed wall, the carefully hand-framed portrait of a Venetian Renaissance lady, splendidly gowned, rubbed elbows with the thumbtacked glossy photo of a Thalstadt matinee idol.

For Sabine was all these things, and more. At times it seemed hardly believable that she, with her lithe beauty and quicksilver ways, could be a child of Grandfather's; it was enough to make one think about those stories in which dwarfs stole a baby from its unguarded cradle and left a fairy-child in its place. Sabine loved paintings and pretty dresses, dances and "deep" discussions; she "adored" Jean Harlow and Anna Karenina; she was going to Berlin and study drama under Max Reinhardt and be a famous actress. If she had let it be known that she would be Amelia Earhart or the queen of Madagascar, Eva would have believed her as staunchly and enthusiastically.

The guest bed in Sabine's room was wide and smooth,

and in it Eva slept under a huge, fluffy eiderdown, floating into its expansive softness as into a white summer cloud. Sabine kept late hours; sometimes Eva woke in what seemed like the middle of the night, blinking her eyes against the sudden stab of light. Sabine was brushing her dark hair before the mirror, her slim curves draped in the folds of her long cotton gown.

"Sabine, talk to me. I'm not asleep!"

In the mirror, Eva watched a frown come to Sabine's forehead. She had been interrupted in an absorbing pastime: viewing herself in the oval frame of the glass with the detached appreciation she might bestow on a favorite work of art in the Thalstadt museum.

"Hush, turn your face to the wall and close your eyes," Sabine said. "You'll wake Grandfather. It's much too late for a little girl to be awake!"

Eva obeyed, contenting herself with making faces behind Sabine's uncivilly turned back. Perhaps it was to compensate for her own junior status among her grown-up sisters and brother that Sabine was forever putting Eva in her place. If she blundered into the room they shared while Sabine was singing "Falling in Love Again" in a throaty Marlene Dietrich voice to the accompaniment of her Gramophone, Sabine would stop with insulting pointedness and search among her records for something "more appropriate"—a scratchy rendition of the "Toy Symphony," perhaps, or a small boy's voice piping "Au Claire de la Lune."

The door to Sabine's room might stand open to Eva, but the pathway to her eventful young woman's life remained heartlessly closed. At its adventure Eva could only guess, through giggled telephone conversations furtively overheard, through the habitually reproachful tone in which Grandmother addressed Sabine, and through Grandfather's suspicious grumblings in the hallway as Sabine slipped past him to keep "an engagement," trailed by a whiff of French perfume.

Occasionally, and to Grandmother's visible relief, Sabine would consent to take Eva along on one of her numerous engagements. "My little niece from Thalstadt," she would explain offhandedly when the beau of the moment came to call. And at his surprised "Sabine Weil an *aunt*? Let's see if the lucky child resembles you at all," Sabine would add with great poise: "You see, my two sisters are really of another generation. As for resemblance, that's for you to judge. Look at her eyes and cheekbones, though —*interessant*, don't you agree?" This last was said in a half-whisper that made Eva hope against hope that the remark might be interpreted as a compliment.

The introduction over, Sabine wasted no further attention on her unwitting chaperone; indeed, by the time they reached the outskirts of town, she had become oblivious of her presence. At the first opportunity, Eva would pull her hand out of Sabine's silently obliging one, hanging back under the pretense of picking flowers, her jealous eye on Sabine's graceful walk—torn between a proprietary pride in Sabine's beauty and an aching despair over her own angular plainness, her unformed child's body, her short black hair without the slightest prospect of curl.

And those young men of Sabine's, whose flattering attentions she coolly accepted as her due, unwilling to make a choice between them and equally unwilling to let even one escape from that gossamer net of brightness and banter and irresistible smiles! It was left for Eva to endure their big-brotherly pats on her mutely resisting shoulder, their patronizing questions about her homework or her hobbies, to which they neither expected nor received a reply. For her to hide behind a frozen mask of sullenness a tongue-tied worship for every one of them: Paul, the dark, moody one who nursed his infatuation with fatalistic fortitude, like a toothache; Erich, the cantor's son, a lanky student of philosophy with whom Sabine discussed serious matters like Psychoanalysis and Assimilation. Or Fredl, free spirit and footloose *Wandervogel*, red-haired and freckled, who took Sabine for day-long excursions into the countryside, whistling under her window in the pale morning sun, rucksack on his back and the inevitable guitar slung over his shirtsleeved shoulder. It was Fredl, Eva decided, who was more recklessly in love with Sabine than any of them; and Eva was not surprised to hear him ask, one glowing evening in July, if Sabine would "wait for him" while he finished his training at the Technical Institute in Thalstadt.

"Wait for you, Fredl? Here in Ettingen?" Sabine said softly, resting her head against Fredl's shoulder as they sat beneath the spreading branches of midsummer trees. Eva, perched on a sawed-off tree trunk to study an anthill with a great show of concentration, at once perked up her ears.

"Would you, Sabine?" Fredl said huskily, and held out his arm to draw her closer.

But Sabine eluded his touch so smoothly that his hand remained suspended for one swift, astonished moment before it sank, defeated, across the strings of his faithful guitar.

"Why does everyone conspire to keep me in this tedious place?" Sabine said, exasperation in her voice. "My father grumbles every time I visit my sister in Thalstadt, for fear I might meet some city slicker with dishonorable intentions. My brother wants me to sit in that stuffy little office at his plant, pounding away at the typewriter. My sister-in-law wants me around to play nursemaid to her baby. My mother wants me to marry one of her lady friends' eligible sons and start having babies of my own."

Fredl gazed into Sabine's angry eyes with that mixture of adulation and amusement she seemed to arouse in him. "I'll tell my mother to make friends with yours, Sabine. She's got an eligible son who happens to be in love with you."

Sabine laughed. Even without looking up, Eva knew how beautiful Sabine looked when she laughed, and how her laughter could make one's day either happy or wretched.

"My mother thinks you're very nice, Fredl," Sabine was saying. "And if we had the same religion . . ."

"*Hiking* is my religion," Fredl said with only a half-smile. "The forest is my church."

Sabine leaned over and lightly kissed him on the cheek. "That's very romantic, Fredl. But you know it isn't the right answer to win the hand of the princess. And *your* family feels the same way—you know that too. Our parents are good people, Fredl, but they're philistines —like everyone else in this town."

"You used to *like* Ettingen," Fredl said. "What's gotten into you? You've changed—every time I come home you're different!"

"I've *outgrown* this place—it's stifling, like all Swabian small towns! Flower pots and factory chimneys, gossip and togetherness—I'll suffocate if I don't get away from it all!"

"We'll move to Thalstadt, Sabine. I'll get work in the city and we'll live there."

"Thalstadt isn't a city, it's just the biggest small town of them all," Sabine said.

Eva could hardly believe her ears, for Sabine always seemed to have a marvelous time when she came to stay over: going to matinees with her snooty Thalstadt friend Margo Stein, or when there was a Garbo film and no one else to go with, even with Eva; watching the soccer games at the Maccabee athletic field; doing the foxtrot and tango all night at the winning team's victory dance in her clinging black taffeta gown, with her escort's red rose pinned to its plunging neckline.

"And I don't want to get married," Sabine was saying. "I want to go to Berlin, where the air is free, where so much is happening: the cabarets, a new kind of painting, of theater—Klee and Kandinsky, Brecht and Weill—"

"Street fighting, strikes," Fredl added laconically. "Political assassinations."

Sabine tossed her dark hair. "Well, aren't there always birth pangs when something new is coming into being? You'd never know it in Ettingen, but out there the old is dying—comformity, convention, the old authoritarian ways—the new is being born." Her dark eyes sparkled. "And in the arts, too, Fredl—in new ways of feeling, perceiving, expressing. In those strange, scary plays of Kaiser and Toller about Man and Machine, in the Expressionists' bold colors and forms, that jazzy "American" sound of *The Three Penny Opera.* . . ."

"What I like is *Bauhaus* architecture and design," Fredl said—in a different tone, it seemed to Eva, from the one he usually took with Sabine. "Gropius' emphasis on line and space and texture and light: on the human dimension." He shrugged. "I'm not sure I like the rest, or even understand it."

"I don't know how much I 'understand' either," Sabine said. "But it's exciting, it's life, and I want to be part of it!" She jumped up and stretched her supple body, flinging her arms wide and arching her back under the flaming sky as if to catch the last rays of the sun. "Don't try to keep me here, Fredl! I've outgrown our songs along with Ettingen."

Fredl clambered to his feet. "I didn't hear you object the last time we were here," he said softly, his guitar counter-pointing the throbbing silence with a mocking chord.

Sabine bit her lip. "Things change, people change; you've said it yourself, Fredl."

He looked so dejected, following Sabine down the hill, that Eva reached for his hand.

"Maybe she'll change *again*, Fredl," she whispered. "Maybe if you wait a while, she'll like you again."

He looked down at her in surprise and gave her hand a little squeeze. "Maybe I should wait for Eva to grow up instead," he said lightly, and with the crook of his bare, sun-warmed arm drew Eva's flushed face toward his own. He held her so close she thought she could count his freckles with her finger, smooth the tousled red hair off his frowning forehead. She caught her breath, expecting something momentous to happen—the crimson sky to fall over her hammering heart, or perhaps, perhaps . . .

But he had already released her and caught up to Sabine, glancing back only once with his old, big-brotherly smile to make sure that she was safely behind them.

All the way home through the dusky fields fragrant with

that ripeness that already intimates autumn and other springs, they did not speak. And Fredl's guitar hung mutely by his side, its bright ribbons accentuating the deepening darkness and the queer sadness in Eva's heart —a sadness no longer searing, somehow, but sweet with a song of its own.

Eva's parents had gone back to Thalstadt to soothe Grandfather Bentheim's feelings of desertion, though he had been perfectly well taken care of by Anna in their absence, with daily dinner invitations from the Upstairs. Eva stayed on to spend another week of her summer vacation in Ettingen. From many visits there each year, her mother's hometown had become as familiar to Eva as Thalstadt. Along its sober gray streets she easily made her way between her grandparents' awning-shaded old house on Ulmer Strasse and the airy apartment on Lindenplatz that was the home of the "younger Weils"—Uncle Lutz, his wife, Tilla, and their baby son, Eli. Uncle Lutz was a printer by trade; he ran a small printing plant that sat in a perpetually muddy field on the outskirts of Ettingen; its ancient clattering presses and inky smells made it a fascinating place to come to visit in Uncle Lutz's little red Opel.

But it was to the apartment on Lindenplatz that Eva loved to go. Aunt Tilla had furnished it with low-slung armchairs and a couch whose springy bent-steel legs and tubular arms felt cool and silken smooth to the touch of Eva's gliding fingers. Everything in the younger Weils' apartment was "modern": the nubby striped weave of the upholstery, the vivid splashes and dashes on the starkly-framed paintings on the wall, the odd-shaped vases and sleek-necked lamps on the glass-topped low tables and chests. Aunt Tilla believed in being modern; she wore her blond hair in a stylish bob with a stylish wave pulled over one eye, and she drove the red Opel as sure-handedly as Uncle Lutz did. Aunt Tilla read books on child psychology; she served strange, "healthful" dishes like mushroom loaf and braised lettuce; she fed Eli vitamins and exercised his limbs in front of the open window in the mild morning air until he squealed with laughter.

In his sun-flooded room, Eva played peekaboo with Eli between the bars of his playpen, delighting in the clumsy touch of his small hand against her cheek. She loved holding him damply on her lap after his nighttime bath, his downy blond hair tickling her lips and his clean baby smells enveloping her face.

"I like Eli *so* much!" she burst out one evening, not wanting to let go of the energetic small body when Aunt Tilla came to put Eli to bed.

Aunt Tilla smiled and gently lifted Eli up into her arms. "I know you do, Eva. Eli is very lucky—he has parents, a whole big family to care for him and help him grow up strong and well. I wish all children could have that."

She tucked Eli into his crib and stood looking down on him for a moment longer. "Sometimes I wonder if *any* child is really safe as long as *one* child suffers in this world," she said softly, flicking on the small nightlight on the dresser before she closed the door behind them.

Back at the old house on Ulmer Strasse, Sabine scoffed when Eva told her about the conversation the following afternoon. They sat on the rusty swing in Grandmother's little front garden, where two old pear trees struggling for space and light already bore their sparse and sour fruit.

"Drawing-room socialists, that's what they are, my brother and Tilla—*Salon-Sozialisten! He* reads the *Simplicissimus* that satirizes the Left, the Right, and the Center and thinks that makes him very avant-garde. *She* got her social conscience from looking at her Käthe Kollwitz drawings, and tries to atone for being middle class by working on committees for needy mothers and children."

Eva remembered the Kollwitz drawings in a folio Aunt Tilla had let her look through one evening when she had slept over. They would not have been easy to forget: small children with harrowed wide eyes, holding up empty dishes begging to be filled; workers' wives, drawn in unsparing strokes of black, their faces marked with anguish and despair; a gaunt young man, his arm flung high in a gesture of pledge and defiance: *"Nie Wieder Krieg!"*— "Never Again War!" It seemed natural and right to her that Aunt Tilla wanted to help mothers and children like these: why had Sabine's voice sounded so scornful when she spoke about it in words of a kind usually reserved for her "intellectual" boy friends like Erich: "social conscience," "atone for being middle class"?

"What's middle class?" Eva asked, trying to make sense of it all.

Sabine set the swing in motion with the tip of her foot. "Well, *we* are, for one thing—our family, most of our friends and acquaintances, I guess. You know—not rich, but comfortably off. People who own family stores, like your father or watchmaker Roeblin across the street from you. Tradesmen like *my* father"—Grandfather Weil sold machinery parts to the farms in the surrounding countryside—"doctors like your old Dr. Neuburger in Thalstadt . . ."

Dr. Neuburger, who took care of all the Bentheims, was a distant relative, whose shuffling walk, soggy cigar, and creased, pessimistic features suddenly assembled themselves on the Ettingen front lawn in an acrid cloud of tobacco smoke as thick as the doctor's Bavarian accent. Dr. Neuburger made little jokes that weren't very funny in a gravelly voice always raspy from smoking too many cigars. He was one of the kindest people Eva knew.

"What's so bad about being middle class?" she persisted.

Sabine thought about it for a moment. "Well, first of all it's boring—nothing ever happens in the middle class. And then I suppose people feel sort of caught in the middle: resented by those less well off, especially when times are bad, and doubly resented if they happen to be Jews." The swing creaked. "And the upper class doesn't like middle-class people either," Sabine went on. "It thinks of them as vulgar upstarts—*nouveau riche*—and doubly so—"

"—If they happen to be Jews!" Eva broke in, trying to show Sabine that she had caught on. It had become a kind of game.

Sabine was not amused. "Does the word anti-Semitism also strike you as funny?" she asked sarcastically.

Eva wasn't sure *how* it struck her. Uncomfortable, even disturbing, and yet—distant. Like earthquakes and erupting volcanoes, it seemed to happen elsewhere, to other people. It had to do with poor Captain Dreyfus shouting *"Je suis innocent!"* through the bars of his cell, as Uschi had described it to her after seeing the movie. With Cossacks ransacking Jewish villages in the czars' Russia, with the word *pogrom*, which sounded ominous yet even more foreign than the French words Uschi had tried to pronounce for her.

Of course there were the Nazis, who blamed everything that went wrong in Germany on the Jews. But Uncle Lutz, serious for once, had said only the day before that Germans were too civilized to "swallow that stuff" and would save their democratic government by voting against the Nazis in the elections for Parliament that day. Uncle Lutz went on to say that he was voting for the Social Democratic Party—"same as my printers at the plant!"—and that—"No offense, Eva,"—her father's small Democratic Party was "high-minded but outdated—nineteenth-century humanism in the machine age."

"What matters, though," he had conceded magnanimously, "is that both parties support the Republic, and so do several others."

Then Uncle Lutz had asked Aunt Tilla if that was liver dumplings for dinner he was smelling, and added, "Thank goodness, nothing *healthy* for a change!" Thinking of it, Eva had to laugh all over again.

Sabine, still immersed in her own thoughts, slipped off the swing, leaving it dangling wildly. "You see, Eva, I put my faith in only *one* group—the free artists! Writers, painters, playwrights—they're outsiders, too, like the Jews. They also stick to their beliefs, suffer for them, are ridiculed, reviled." She broke an unripe pear off a low-hanging branch, bit into it, made a wry face and tossed the gnarled green fruit up in the air. "Maybe *someday*, when Germany is ready for its artists, it might even be ready for its Jews!"

"Sabine, save the dramatics for Max Reinhardt!" Uncle

Lutz called out teasingly, coming through the garden gate to pay his parents a visit.

But he was not really in a jocular mood. He opened up the afternoon paper he was carrying under his arm and showed Sabine the headlines. The Nazis had gotten many more votes in yesterday's elections and were now the largest party in the Reichstag, the German parliament. Of course, Uncle Lutz said, there were many parties, large and small, Left, Right, and Center—and *most* people had *not* voted for the Nazis. Anyway, there was always another election!

Uncle Lutz added with satisfaction that in Thalstadt and Ettingen, and in Swabia as a whole, the Nazis had not done nearly so well as in some other parts of the country. Still, Eva thought, following Sabine into the house arm in arm with Uncle Lutz, it was good to know that Sabine had so much faith in her "free artists." If things ever got bad for the Jews in Germany, as they once had in France, there surely would be Germans like Zolà, the great French writer, who would put a stop to it all by saying, "*J'accuse!*"

That was the part of the movie Uschi had liked the best.

8 ✡✡✡

Sabine, hoping to save up money for Berlin, was pounding the typewriter at Uncle Lutz's office, and Eva was reading her way through Sabine's bookcase instead of playing "with those nice Hanauer girls down the street," as Grandmother kept suggesting.

"Why don't you take Eva for a walk tomorrow, Simon?" Grandmother asked Grandfather one evening. "I don't want her to go home to her mother all pale from being indoors. Take her out in the fresh air a bit, show her around Ettingen."

And though Grandfather pretended surprise at the notion that anything in Ettingen might be of possible interest to a "fine lady from the provincial capital," he announced early at breakfast the next morning that he was waiting for Eva to get ready.

The August haze was barely lifting from the rooftops of the sleepy town. Holding Eva's hand in the cool hollow of his great parched palm, Grandfather strode beside her, tall and remote in his impenetrable silence. Here and there across the cobbled streets, another early riser waved a greeting, and Grandfather returned the gesture with a curt nod or a muttered *Grüss Gott*. Once, long after the passerby had disappeared around a corner, Grandfather cleared his throat: "That was Heiner Gerstle," he told Eva as if she were a grown-up. "A hard-working farmer and a *rechtschaffener Mann*."

"A righteous man"—she had heard him use the phrase with the same note of approval before. On his slow Swabian tongue the words took on an austere grandeur that seemed to Eva at once like that of the Bible and of old regional legends. She saw no contradiction between the two: was not Grandfather's furrowed face like the medieval woodcuts of peasant faces in Sabine's art books; were not his brooding, troubled eyes the eyes of Amos and Ezekiel?

Nor had it taken her long to perceive that "righteousness," to Grandfather, implied more than a decent way of taking care of one's family, one's livestock, and one's land: old regional and biblical virtues of industry, integrity and thrift. "He does not discriminate," Grandfather would add occasionally, referring to one of his townsmen. Discriminate as to what was never formalized in words, but Eva was by now old enough, and wise enough, to understand exactly.

Grandfather had turned onto the high road that led past the railroad station and followed the gleaming tracks into the open country beyond the town. Farm wagons passed them, piled high with hay on which the dew of the meadows still glistened. After a while, Grandfather slowed his brisk stride and walked on leisurely, humming under his breath, a bit self-consciously at first, but breaking into full-throated song at last. They were a singing family, the Weils; and Eva, her fleet soprano taking wing from Grandfather's true, rough-hewn baritone, offered a silent prayer of thanks that she, a Bentheim, had by a happy turn of fortune come by her mother's familial gift of song.

Grandfather cleared his throat. "And now," he announced solemnly, "we shall sing the aria from *The Postilion de Longjumeau*, prize song of Royal Swabian Opera Singer Sontheim, who was my father's uncle, as you know!"

And he began at once, tossing his hand in the best operatic tradition: "Friends, come and listen to my stoooory / About a fine young postilion . . ."

"Postilion!" Eva fell in promptly in place of the chorus.

Grandfather gave her a sidelong glance. "Good, Eva. It pleases me to hear you sing with me. Sontheim's most celebrated role . . ."

"Then you would say he was *famous*, your great-uncle Sontheim?" Eva loved to hear Grandfather tell about his favorite kinsman, whose portrait hung over the piano in her grandparents' living room: a mustached gentleman in open shirt collar, wearing a flowing silk scarf. None of her tone-deaf Bentheim relations could boast of a Royal Opera Singer on their family tree, though Ella had lamely proposed a distant cousin who played on the Bavarian champion soccer team.

"Was Sontheim famous?" Grandfather scoffed, precisely as she had intended. "He was one of the foremost opera singers of his time! The King himself, the public, and the music world acclaimed him as the *Kaiser* of the tenors!"

They were approaching the bend in the road where the rails veered sharply toward the distant chimneys of factory towns to the north. Beyond the tracks lay the small village where Grandfather had been born and raised.

"The trains don't stop here any longer, Eva," Grandfather said at the crossing. "The village has grown old, just as I have. The young people went off to the cities to work in the factories and mills. Time and the trains have left the village behind."

They crossed the rails humming faintly beneath their steps and walked along a wheel-furrowed road. It had grown warm; the dry air smelled of hay and wildflowers, spiced with the pungent odors of dung; above the dozing farmyards, the stubby steeple of the village church thrust its plain cross into the gilded sky. Gradually, the road narrowed into a winding lane. A high stone wall rose to the left, covered with thin green tendrils of climbing vine. Hedgeroses poured their sweet fragrance into the gathering heat.

With an air of mystery, Grandfather raised Eva in his arms and let her peer across the wall. Beyond a dark row of cypresses stiffly silhouetted against the shimmering sky stood an old house. Its windows were shuttered and the steps leading to the bolted door grown over with ivy, as if it had stood lonely and vacant for a long, long time.

"It is the country synagogue, Eva, where Sontheim sang as a young boy," her grandfather said in an almost reverent tone. "Here the old cantor discovered the promise in the lad's untrained voice. Here, too, the story goes, he persuaded the father—a pious man with many children and few means—to let the boy take singing lessons in the capital. Sontheim always remembered. My father often recalled how his uncle, then in his best years and at the peak of his career, would visit here on the High Holy Days and lead the congregation in song."

They walked on slowly. Soon they came to a fence with an iron gate that gave way briefly, creakily, under her grandfather's probing hand. He did not take her farther, but in the shadows beyond the fence Eva perceived a great stillness, a coolness of motionless leaves. Along the moss-grown path, the weathered gravestones stood solitary and remote, their Hebrew inscriptions faded and whittled smooth by the winds and rains of the passing years.

"My father, David," Grandfather murmured at Eva's side, his voice scarcely louder than the hum of the bees and the whisper of the grass. "My mother, Hannah, may she rest in peace. My grandfather, and *his* grandfather, Simon, son of Michael from the town of Weil."

She pressed her face against the cool, dark bars. "*Your* grandfather's *great*-grandfather?"

"Yes, child, that was a very long time ago. And yet, once before—centuries before Michael Weil, before this *kever ovos*, resting place of our forebears—Jews lived in Ettingen and the village. Our martyrs' scrolls tell us so; their sojourn here has left no other trace. In 1348 the Black Death came, and those of our people who survived the plague were slain by their neighbors for having caused it."

"For having *caused* it?" It made no sense to her.

Grandfather sat down on a bench in sudden exhaustion, as if his walk had taken him not merely the few miles from town but on an infinitely longer journey, a journey not in distance but in time.

"We had poisoned the wells, they were told. We Jews, who hold life sacred above all else, had poisoned the wells! And they rose up against us, the desperate and the deceived, the cruel and covetous, to cleanse their souls and cancel their debts in the blood of Abel. How many were there—man, woman, and child—who died *al kiddush ha-Shem*, to sanctify His Name, in Ettingen and hundreds of villages and towns? We do not know; only that they were here and that their names became like ashes in the wind. . . ."

It was quiet and peaceful under the swaying trees. A peasant boy, his bare feet kicking up little clouds of dust, was leading an unwilling goat up the road. Somewhere a rooster crowed, halfheartedly, as if it were already too late in the day to make a row.

In 1348, her grandfather had said. She could hardly imagine how long ago 1348 was; but if it were taught in school, it would come before Frederick the Great, before Duke Ernst of Swabia, before the Thirty Years' War, before the Peasant Wars—even before Columbus! She shut her eyes and tried to see those others, those who had lived and died on this same sunny earth in that long-vanished year. But they would not rise to her bidding; shrouded in time, they remained nameless, faceless, their lives and violent deaths beyond the safe realm of reality. She wondered, vaguely perturbed, why Grandfather had spoken to her at all of such dark and dreadful happenings—the kind her father would consider "not meant for the ears of a child."

But as she glanced at her grandfather's face, it seemed to be *he* who needed reassurance.

She touched his hand. "Don't worry, Grandfather. If anyone in Ettingen were to talk about poisoned wells today, nobody would believe him! Remember Sontheim," she added, struck by a cheering thought. "How people loved and honored him, even the king of Swabia himself!"

Startled, Grandfather blinked his eyes and shook out his rumpled trouser legs, almost as if she had roused him from sleep. "Yes, Eva, these are different times. We are *citizens* now, like the others, protected by German law. And laws are a beginning: society's pledge to itself to seek to do better. But as for Sontheim," he went on darkly, "he whom they call the Swabian Caruso, for whom the Vienna orchestra laid down its instruments to join in the applause —he, too, was made to drink the bitter cup. There were those who never forgave him for having served his musical apprenticeship in a country synagogue, assisting the village cantor—as if the stream of German music had been sullied by this cross-current from another source. Had not Wagner himself declared that Jews, by nature, could not create great art? And was it not the gossip of the capital that he had publicly insulted Sontheim in the dining room of their hotel? Sontheim never again sang Wagner after that shameful incident."

Why was it, Eva thought, that Grandfather, who knew his dates so well, remembered only those that brought him pain? There he sat, his chin morosely buried in his palm, fretting the lovely morning with hurtful memories. Even to her, who was only a child, there was something wasteful —almost, she thought disloyally, something a little laughable—about the way he sat and nursed his ancient grudges.

"As long as it is only Wagner!" she burst out flippantly. "I don't much like his music anyway. It is too loud."

Grandfather shot her a withering glance. "Ah, Wagner cannot be disparaged, my child!" His hands swept forward, summoning unseen instruments. "A painter in sound, Eva—a stirrer, a shaker, a reveler in human emotion."

He shrugged; the unheard music had ended. "But also a

hater, as so many others, the great and the humble, now as then. Sometimes when I walk through the streets of the town or stop at the farms, I can see it in the blankness of their faces or hear it in the words they fail to speak."

He leaned forward and carefully picked up a windblown leaf. "Do you see the brown spots on the green, Eva? We call it the leaf blight; it is a bad disease. Trees, too, can have diseases, like people and animals. At first, only a handful of leaves are stricken, but if they are not treated and cured, in time the whole forest will suffer and die."

His eyes scanned the dazzling sky. "It is getting late. I am expected at the Lehmbach farm before noon. Remind me to speak to the caretaker on the way home. Perhaps the tree can still be saved."

9 ⚘⚘⚘

On Saturday afternoons during the warm season, the Thalstadt military band gave its weekly concert on the Schlossplatz. While brassy tunes blared from the pillared pavilion in the center of the square, Grandfather Bentheim took in the sun on one of the crowded benches and tapped out the rhythm with his cane, brisk marches and lilting waltzes being the only kind of music he approved of. Uschi and Eva sat on the pavilion steps, sifting into their white-pleated skirts the white and fragrant chestnut petals that drifted from the tall trees like a fine swirl of snow. Between the Radetzky March and the Blue Danube, a momentary hush sank over the square; only the fountain rose silently, fell silently, into the luminous sea of noon. The Marble Column glinted in the sunlight: poised on its crown, the Angel of Peace suspended its golden wings and spread its down-turned, blessing palms. It was a perfect moment, until the trombonist unfeelingly took his instrument apart and let a thin stream of water (the girls never referred to it by its real nature and name) trickle to the stone floor of the pavilion. Uschi and Eva stared wide-eyed in mesmerized disgust. It was the high point of the performance.

After the concert, when they had watched the musicians pack up their instruments and fold away their stands, they made their way toward Grandfather's bench, bracing themselves for what lay ahead. Everyone on the Schlossplatz knew Grandfather, it seemed, and it was necessary to respond to a ceaseless flow of tiresome adult questions and observations. At last, after they had duly told their first names a dozen times and dubiously accepted as many compliments on their behavior during the concert, Grandfather rose smoothly, fixed the stiff brim of his straw hat, and twirled his cane in a gesture of parting. Uschi and Eva curtsied hastily, relieved at their escape and yet not unpleasantly aware that Grandfather was a person of substance in Thalstadt. Slowly, sedately, each holding on to one of Grandfather's arms, they walked across the Schlossplatz. Only when they knew themselves safely beyond the scrutiny of watchful eyes did they begin to skip ahead or lag behind—to stray into the cool and secret bypaths of the park, from where they reemerged noisily at the gate, with stolen dandelions hidden behind their backs and telltale grass stains on their rumpled skirts.

Spring passed into summer. One Saturday the blazing candles on the wild chestnut trees stood in their purest, whitest fullness. The next weekend they were gone, scorched under the first torrid breath of summer heat. For a few Saturdays, there was only the deep satiate green of the leaves overhead, the silent stirring of branches in the faint, drowsy breeze. Then the first tiny fruits obligingly dropped to the ground, their skins still pale and tender,

downy like peaches and supple to the probing touch of their
fingers, with only the merest hint of the growing kernel
beneath. As the weeks passed the color deepened, the
circumference widened; the skin toughened and bristled
with short, supple spikes. At last, stretched beyond limits
by the urge of the expanding core within, the taut skin
burst open and the glossy brown chestnuts lay ripely in the
palms of their hands: at once fruition and promise, autumn
no more than an interval between one springtime and
another. And time, marking its gentle passage by the
chestnut trees, was the time of their childhood, without
beginning and seemingly without end.

One late August afternoon, as they were leaving the park
under a gathering phalanx of rain-boding clouds, a long,
lean shadow fell over Grandfather's short, upright one, and
a restraining hand caught his elbow. He turned, indignantly, his lips already pursed for a caustic reproof at the
intrusion on his leisurely walk. Instead, a flush of recognition spread over his face.

"Herr Hallenbeck!" he said curtly, touching his hand to
the stiff brim of his straw hat. His eyes, faintly amused,
faintly wary, scanned the smooth-shaven face before him.
"And to what circumstance, I wonder, do I owe the
honor?"

Uschi and Eva exchanged a significant glance. So this
was Herr S. Hallenbeck, the owner of the big department
store across the square. Herr Hallenbeck, whose white-
walled villa overlooked Thalstadt from the heights of the
Buchberg!

"Well, I have finally caught up with you, Herr Bentheim," the tall man said in clipped North German speech.

"Your sons have led me to believe that you were all but inaccessible these days. A pity, Herr Bentheim; the proposition I have been seeking to make to you would prove of benefit to both of us."

Grandfather said nothing. He walked ahead, swinging his cane, his stride curiously buoyant for a man of his years. Herr Hallenbeck easily kept pace. His gloved hand resting lightly on Grandfather's arm, he simply fell in step—past the medieval turrets of the Old Castle, past the Memorial Church, and across the drafty Schillerplatz with the weathered statue of the poet at its center.

Herr Hallenbeck pointed toward a vacant bench. "Why not talk it over right here, Herr Bentheim? If these charming young ladies will spare us a moment of their time?"

Uschi and Eva barely stifled a most unladylike giggle. But perhaps Grandfather was more impressed, for with a shrug and a passing glance at the sky, he followed Herr Hallenbeck's unfaltering lead and sat down next to him on the bench. The girls did likewise—choosing the opposite end of the bench, where they might hope to remain both inconspicuous and within earshot of the conversation.

A sudden gust of wind swept a flurry of dust across the square.

"*Jawohl*, Herr Hallenbeck," Grandfather said quietly. "I am well aware of the conversations that have been held between your sons and mine. I imagine it is only a mistaken, but in view of my age a quite understandable wish to shield me from business matters that has prevented my sons from having you meet with me personally, as you requested. But there is no reason why we should not come to an understanding this afternoon. Especially since my decision has long been reached and is beyond further discussion."

Herr Hallenbeck smoothed the pigskin gloves he was carrying. "Your sons have indicated as much, Herr Bentheim. If your decision is still negative, however, I can only advise you to reconsider. For my part, I am quite prepared to go beyond our initial offer."

He crossed his long legs and laid his arm along the back of the bench in a gesture of easy cordiality. "We must expand, Herr Bentheim. We are bursting at the seams, and since our acquisition of the Optician Maerz house some time ago, we have no way to turn but east."

He leaned forward and, picking up grandfather's cane, outlined a figure five in the gritty dust. "I am offering you five hundred thousand Marks for your house and your business, Herr Bentheim."

Uschi and Eva caught their breath. They did not really know how much money that many Marks might be. But remembering the great basket of red carnations Herr Hallenbeck had sent for Grandfather's birthday, they concluded at once that he was doubtless as magnanimous as he was wealthy. They looked at each other in sudden apprehension. What if Grandfather chose to say yes? Where would they go? Not all the money in the world could ever buy another house like Grandfather's for them to live in!

Grandfather nodded thoughtfully, a quizzical smile brushing the corners of his mouth under the crisp white mustaches. "Herr Hallenbeck, you are most persuasive. When I came to Thalstadt as a young apprentice more years ago than I care to recall, I had scarcely more than five Mark pieces in my pocket. And I am not averse to admitting that when I first opened my little shop, it was on considerably less than five thousand Marks, plus what I like to think of as my good name. While the firm has certainly flourished since, particularly under the able guidance of my elder son, I must say in all fairness that your previous offer would have been quite acceptable—if we wanted to sell."

Uschi and Eva heaved a deep sigh of relief.

But Herr Hallenbeck was not to be put off so quickly. "Then why *not* sell, Herr Bentheim? Need I remind you that in addition to your deservedly fine reputation, you are also known as an astute and farsighted man of affairs? If you reject my offer and force us to look elsewhere in the locality for a plot on which to build our new wing, your firm, a modest family enterprise, will face increasing competition from our corporate, up-to-date department store. Why not make a fresh beginning with the capital resources you stand to gain—in Munich, Frankfurt, perhaps Berlin?"

Grandfather's hand crumbled a stale piece of bread left wedged between the slats of the bench by a previous visitor. He scattered the crumbs and watched a flock of droopy pigeons pick at them desultorily.

"Why do men arrive at decisions, Herr Hallenbeck? Not necessarily because they are the wisest but because they seem right, I suppose. So it seems right for us to take our chances and stay. This town has been home to me for more than sixty years; my sons and my daughter, and their children in turn, have never known another. And without wanting to call into question my reputation as a seasoned businessman, there *are* considerations other than purely practical ones: a certain human obligation toward our employees, perhaps unable to find new situations in these uncertain times. Even if you should be able to make room for them in your organization, there are my tenants, who have been my neighbors for a great many years and whose homes would be sacrificed to our mutual gain."

He rubbed his hands to brush off a last dry crumb. "I'm sorry, Herr Hallenbeck, but I do wish you would respect my decision. I can assure you that it is fruitless to try to sway us."

A few scattered raindrops fell heavily on the bench, seeping thirstily into the parched wooden slats. The clouds hung low; in the false twilight, the Schiller monument stood dipped in red.

Herr Hallenbeck blinked warily into the slanting sun. "*Mein lieber* Herr Bentheim, what I shall say to you now may be received in anger. If I risk saying it nonetheless, perhaps you will allow me that I am placing your best interests even above my own."

Grandfather pursed his lips and raised his smooth white eyebrows over narrowed eyes. It was a sign of danger with which the girls were only too well acquainted. Herr Hallenbeck went on undaunted, however, unaware that he was venturing on hazardous ground.

"Herr Bentheim, you and I belong to the old school. We are a dying generation. A new wind is blowing in Germany; we may not like its force or its direction, but I believe it is already too powerful to be opposed. I shall be frank to say that there are those among my colleagues in the business world, yes, even within my closest family circle, who feel it is a good thing. I am speaking of those who are no longer willing to share the German market and the German Mark with merchants in a . . . more exposed position, and who will readily support a movement that turns the anger of the unemployed and the dispossessed against a . . . certain segment of the population."

The square lay deserted now. Even the pigeons had left the wilting crumbs and flown off somewhere into the low gray sky. The clouds bore a sulfur cast, and it was hot, with the massed, laden heat that carries the seeds of storm.

"If I were in your shoes, Herr Bentheim," Herr Hallenbeck said, "I would advise my family to leave for firmer shores as quickly as affairs could be arranged."

Eva and Uschi stared at each other in disbelief, then turned their startled faces toward Grandfather. He did not disappoint them.

He doffed his hat in the direction of the monument. " 'Save thyself, Wallenstein!' " he said in his ironic voice, quoting from Schiller's play. "From *what*, Herr Hallenbeck? Unlike that Imperial general's, who served two masters and was in turn betrayed by both, *my* conscience is entirely clear. No one bears us ill will: we're Thalstadt burghers and businessmen as any others on the square, except that Bentheim and Sons stays closed for two additional holidays each fall. Your concern is appreciated, Herr Hallenbeck, but rest assured it is entirely misplaced. Perhaps from the heights of the Buchberg, among the lofty company you keep, one's vision of Thalstadt tends to get out of focus. Perhaps a change of air, Herr Hallenbeck— Italy, France—or merely a new set of spectacles. Optician Maerz, whose house and business you bought out last year, has opened a small shop on Wertherstrasse. I'm sure he would oblige."

As if heaven were on his side, the clouds split and a downpour of rain whipped the square, relieving Herr Hallenbeck of the necessity of making a reply.

PART ✦✦✦ THREE

The Face on the Kiosk

1 ✿✿✿

The leaves were turning.

From her seat by the window, Eva watched autumn move in on the schoolyard below. It came surreptitiously: a stranger loosing the latch of the gate by night to slip in under the cover of dark, always retreating the next morning under the lingering warmth of the September sun, but leaving everywhere first traces of his furtive calls. The dahlias glowed; in nature study Frau Ackermann dropped beechnuts and acorns on their desks, reminding them that the oak was Germany's national tree.

"And like the sturdy oak," she added quietly, "our German *Volk* has weathered many a storm."

Raising his hand, Klaus Herzog remarked in his ponderous way that the Black Forest was mainly pines. "It's cool and dark there, even in August, and pine needles fall from the trees and make the ground feel soft under your feet."

Frau Ackermann smiled her appreciation. "We can tell where Klaus spent his vacation this year!"

And with some minutes left before the bell, they talked once more of the past summer holidays already tinged with that faint aura of regret for things beyond recall: Klaus and his father on their hiking tour; the Goetzes mountain climbing in the Bavarian Alps; Monika on the Lueneburger Heath, visiting high-born relatives with hyphenated noble names.

Horst had been farther than anyone—on the island of Rügen in the Baltic Sea. "Where the cliffs are made of chalk," he boasted, stretching his hand toward the ceiling to show how tall and steep the cliffs rose from the sea.

And then Horst did a curious thing.

He leaned across the boys' row, and staring at Eva from under his thick blond lashes, said in a loud whisper: "But only *real* Germans are allowed on Rügen!"

She felt her cheeks grow hot as if he had slapped her.

For a long moment, she waited for it to happen: the ripple of laughter rising from the benches to drown out Horst's spiteful words; Frau Ackermann tapping her ruler against the blackboard to have him repeat the Three Things she would Absolutely Not Abide. Or hadn't they *heard*? Renate, next to Eva, whose cautious sideways glance she felt rather than saw; Diete, two rows ahead, studiedly turning her head for a pretended look at the clock; Frau Ackermann, writing the day's assignment on the blackboard?

With an effort, Eva made herself stare back at Horst until he looked away with a shrug and a sheepish grin. She drew a deep breath: No, she would not be like Grandfather Weil, brooding on ancient slights and injuries. Turning her back on Horst, she picked up her pen and copied down the assignment.

"So quiet today, Eva?" Frau Ackermann said at the door,

watching her class walk down the hall in orderly fashion.

Eva shifted her books. Now, perhaps, Frau Ackermann would explain—or better still, explain *away*—what Horst had whispered in class, would assure her that she had already called Horst aside and warned him about hurting someone's feelings.

But the teacher, one hand on the polished doorknob, was searching her ample brown pocketbook for the classroom key.

"What a marvelous afternoon," Frau Ackermann murmured absently, surveying her bright and ordered domain with a parting glance of satisfaction. Then she firmly shut the door on another day, on the thing that hung in the stillness beyond the wall, like dust clinging to the shaft of September sun over the empty benches.

Not everyone, it turned out the next day, had been away during the summer. There had been no vacation for the Hubers. Anton's father had lost his job with the Dietz auto works on the Neckar, along with many other men for whom there suddenly no longer had been work.

"But we went swimming in the Neckar every afternoon, my father and I," Anton said quickly into the backwash of sympathy in the classroom. "Except on the days when my Father had to go *stempeln*," he blurted, catching himself too late, and bolted to his seat, his face afire, to study a snow-capped landscape in his geography book.

Stempeln. Eva recognized the word Anton had carelessly revealed to his classmates, which made some hide their laughter behind cupped hands and others fidget awkwardly in their seats, almost as if they were trying to make a little space around Anton, to separate themselves from some creeping contagion. *Stempeln.* It was one of those words, like *inflation*, like *unemployment*, the *lost territories*, and *the times*, which had come to mark the air, signposts of her childhood and steppingstones to things to come, casting long shadows on the familiar landscape of her life.

"Look at the unemployed going *stempeln* for their dole!" Diete Goetz had said one afternoon last winter as she and Eva and Renate walked past the unemployment office on their way to the skating pond in the park. "Getting their cards stamped, or something of the sort, so they can't cheat on their insurance money."

There had been a long line of people outside the gray government building that ice-blue day, waiting in the cold winter sun—men mostly, but also women with children by the hand, huddled into the scant comfort of their thread-bare coats. Passing them by, her glittering skates dangling like silver from her mittened hand, Eva had looked away, ashamed for Diete and ashamed as well for her own new red birthday sweater and scarf, feeling the glance of wind-stung, disillusioned eyes through the layers of wool on her back.

A young boy in a field-gray soldier's jacket whose sleeves reached almost to his fingertips walked alongside the bleak column, pressing leaflets into reluctant hands. "Unemployed meeting tonight!" His voice rang over the defeated silence on the square. "Seven o'clock at the Trade Union Hall!"

"Don't take that stuff!" Diete called out sharply as Renate reached for one of the wind-ruffled sheets.

She caught the leaflet in the frozen air and crumpled it into a ball.

"Go keep your Red propaganda!" Diete pitched the ball at the face of the boy; perhaps not unaccustomed to surprise attacks, he managed to dodge it neatly. To Eva's secret satisfaction, he even managed a tight smile.

"And what do you call *them*—Red propaganda, too?" He pointed to the shuffling line behind them.

Pushing past him, Diete muttered something about Communist traitors; but Renate, with a sudden surge of belated rebellion, stopped to pick up the crumpled piece of paper and smoothed it out against the wall of the building.

" 'Workers, Defend Your Unions!' " Eva read over her shoulder. " 'National Socialism Means War, Not Bread!' "

"What did I tell you—Red propaganda!" Diete cried, snatching the leaflet for a second time and ripping it into bits.

Now another cold season was drawing near. Eva thought of the boy in the soldier's jacket. Would Anton, too, shiver in the long line this winter? She hoped not; one could tell at a glance that even a summer's swimming in the Neckar had not made him stronger, and that he worked harder than he should to safeguard his grades and his scholarship at school.

She had suspected that things were not going well for Anton since early last summer, the day of the class excursion to Schloss Monrépos. For that outing, Inge Beisswanger had stuffed so many wurst sandwiches into her knapsack that she was finally forced to give up, eyeing her last salami on pumpernickel bread with mixed regret and revulsion. While Frau Ackermann chatted with the guide about the old dukes of Swabia and their extravagant courts, which sought to rival the splendor of those of the

French kings across the Rhine, Inge pushed the paper bag with the uneaten sandwich under a marble bench in the castle yard.

Suddenly Frau Ackermann, who seemed to see things through the blue cornflowers at the back of her stylish straw hat, whipped around. In a clipped voice she asked Inge to *desist* from littering the castle grounds and from wasting good food when, as she very well knew, other Germans were going hungry. Contritely, Inge fumbled under the bench and came up red-faced: the lunch bag was gone! Frau Ackermann shot a sharp glance in the direction of the boys, but evidently decided that historic Schloss Monrépos was not the place for a showdown over some childish prank.

Calmly, though with an edge to her voice, she announced that it was time to leave and led them back at a brisk pace under the tall trees the duke had planted two centuries earlier to line a bridle path for his favorite French ballerina. It had, indeed, grown late; the bus driver was honking his horn impatiently as they stepped out of the woods. Running toward the bus next to Anton, Eva noticed a curious bulge under his carefully buttoned jacket and an unmistakable scent of salami about his small, slight person. She managed shrewdly to squeeze into the seat next to him, but even so she worried about him until he got off at his stop.

The next day she drew Renate aside in the gym; perched on the footbench used for obstacle races—dark silky head bent close to flaxen, primly braided one—they plotted their strategy. They would take turns bringing double lunches to school and, under the pretext that he must save them from a parental scolding, trick Anton into eating the extra portion.

They overacted badly the first day. But Anton never seemed to suspect their game and in a short time became as accomplished at playing his part as they had become at theirs.

"And what about you, Helga?" Frau Ackermann was saying, just as the bell began to ring. "Surely you spent your summer in Saxony again, on your grandparents' farm?" she prompted in her brightest voice, determined to end the session on a cheerier note.

But little Helga Boehm shook her head with the two short brown pigtails. "Grandfather lost his farm, Frau Ackermann," she said in her drawn-out Saxon. She looked about the room to make sure her words had left an impression and added sagely, "Mother says Grandfather just couldn't hold out any longer."

Frau Ackermann suppressed a sigh. "Yes, children, our country has come upon bad times. Pray God things will take a turn for the better before long. . . ."

At home, too, there was talk of "the times." Often, in the evening, Eva's father would put down his newspaper and walk to the window, scanning the gathering autumnal dusk beyond the first lights flaring up in the square. She wondered what it was that troubled her father. Owning a store would seem to make it unlikely for anyone to put him out of work, as had been done to Herr Huber; and there was no sign of want in the meals her mother set on the dinner table. Yet even at night, when she was secretly reading in bed instead of going to sleep, she could hear the talk in the other room turn to "the times," with an undercurrent of apprehension.

"My former colleagues in the Reichstag have forgotten the workingmen in the factories who sent them to Berlin to speak for them," Herr Gerber said in his broad Swabian dialect. He laughed curtly, his cheerless laughter ending in a fit of coughing. "Concessions to Hindenburg's landowner friends; concessions to the industrialists. They are equivocating the Republic into its grave!" he added, catching his breath.

Herr Gerber was a war comrade of Eva's father—a large, burly man who spoke and moved heavily and always carried a neatly pressed handkerchief in his breast pocket, with which he would dab his forehead on even the coolest of days. Herr Gerber insisted that he had acquired this habit during his brief but heated tenure as a Reichstag delegate right after the war "when the workers still had the sense to send up men willing to do a little sweating for their cause."

But Eva knew differently. During the war, her father had explained, their battallion had come under a gas attack, and the poisonous fumes had permanently impaired Herr Gerber's health. Perhaps it was the acid in his lungs that put the bite into Herr Gerber's peasant speech and the bitterness into his field-gray eyes.

"Equivocating the Republic into its grave." Without truly understanding the words, Eva caught the chilling quality of the phrase, evoking moss and stone and the dark pungent smell of earth freshly dug. . . .

One day last spring, passing the newspaper kiosk on Friedrichstrasse on her way home from piano lessons, she had noticed a cartoon tacked up between the *Thalstadt Guardian* and the Nazis' *N. S. Kurier*. Cartoons were hard to understand; usually, Eva would puzzle over them, trying on meanings, never certain even when she had made her final choice that they fit. Yet if she gave up in exasperation and went to her father for help, the answer more often than not turned out to be so obvious that she could scarcely see how anyone, even she, could have missed it.

This time, however, the meaning fairly leaped at her from the newspaper kiosk! A man wearing a somber, flowing cape was riding his horse through a windswept night, holding a sick and frightened boy in his arms. It was, of course, the father in Goethe's poem, *The Erl King*, though the wording underneath the drawing had been cleverly changed from Goethe's. The frantic father here was Chancellor Brüning, and the delirious child he was desperately trying to save from the Erl King—Death—was the Republic!

She hardly could wait to tell her father about the cartoon. But her father nodded glumly. "I would hope Herr Brüning knows better than to rely on a horse," he said drily. "Hitler travels by airplane. And even more speedily by loudspeaker and film. He's reaching hundreds of thousands in a single day."

Not many weeks later, at the end of May, Frau Ackermann remarked in school one morning that Chancellor Brüning had lost his office and that Reichspresident von Hindenburg had appointed Herr von Papen to the post.

"Herr Brüning is gone but his child is still alive!" Eva said, wittily she thought, that evening after dinner when her father picked up his paper with the big red headline.

Her father said nothing. After a while he put down the paper and walked to the window, watching the slow spring twilight descend on the square. He stood for a long time, drawing in the cool evening air in which asphalt and exhaust mingled with the green and growing scents of the park.

"Yes, tonight it is still alive," he said softly at last. And he stood in the waning light until dusk fell and the first street lamps flared up in the square.

A flurry of laughter rose in the living room next door. There was the comforting *cling-clang* of spoons against the fragile cups, and the warm, tartly sweet fragrance of newly baked apple cake.

"Coffee, Herr Gerber?" her mother's voice asked just beyond the wall.

Eva, dozing off over her book, sleepily switched off the lamp. In the morning, she would wheedle Anna into slipping a piece of cake into her school lunch. A large one—Anton was fond of apple cake.

2 ✲✲✲

"Father, I speak now Eng-lish to you," Ella chanted slowly and patiently, punctuating each syllable with a tap of her foot on the living-room floor.

"Fahser, Ispeek nowinglish toyoo!" Uschi and Eva repeated in parrot-fashion, hanging their heads.

It was early October, an unusually mild and sunny autumn for Thalstadt, and Anna predicted the best apple harvest the Remstal had ever seen. Through the open window over the square, the sounds of Sunday morning drifted into the room—voices, footsteps, the thin peal of St. Christopher's and the sonorous boom from the Memorial Church tower. Eva wished she could have gone along to the station to meet the American visitors instead of sitting here, a virtual prisoner to Ella's impossible consonants. But at the last moment Grandfather had decided that only the grown-ups should go.

"Fahser, Ispeek nowinglish toyoo."

If only Grandfather's brothers had emigrated to a country, where people spoke *French*, which Eva had just begun to study in school.

Ella interrupted their mournful recitation. "*Lisp* a little, why can't you!" Her tongue darted to her front teeth in demonstration. "*Fahser* won't do—it's Fa-*ther!*"

Uschi came up with a comforting thought. "Why bother teaching us the English for 'father', Ella? All we really need is the word for 'cousin.'"

Ella sighed. "'Father' is *not* the only English word pronounced with a lisp. I merely picked it for you to practice on. And wait till we get to *W*, and the tricky English *R*, not to speak of—"

Eva's mother hurried into the room and ran a last glance of scrutiny over the furniture. "There they are now!" she said nervously over a mounting din of footsteps and voices in the stairwell.

Uschi and Eva looked at one another in sudden relief. The strange new voices in the hall spoke *German*—an awkward, muffled German, to be sure, as if it came filtered through mouthfuls of Aunt Gustl's hot Bavarian *knödels;* but it seemed less than likely now that they would have to demonstrate their lisps, the *W*, and the dread English *R!*

Eva's father, followed by the Upstairs and Aunt Hanni, ushered the visitors into the room. There was a swarm of kisses and embraces and bilingual exclamations, and only Grandfather's shrewdly delayed entrance unscrambled the Americans sufficiently so that each one could be seen separately.

The gaunt, gray-haired man who wore a little corded button in his ear would be Cousin Arthur, son of the eldest of Grandfather's four brothers who had left the Rhineland in their youth to seek their fortune in America. Eva had heard their story many times. It was, as all such stories ought to be, tinged with sadness and romance.

Daniel, the youngest of the four, had died in Boston of

influenza the winter following his arrival. He had been Grandfather's favorite brother, a husky country lad with red cheeks who looked "as if he could pull trees out of the ground." Even now, more than half a century later, his lonely death in a faraway city of strangers was never to be referred to in Grandfather's presence.

Joseph, the second brother, had drifted west and finally settled down with his American wife in some sleepy prairie town that no one back home had ever heard of.

"And there the story ends," Eva's mother would say regretfully. "Joseph's old father could not forgive him for marrying outside his faith, and Joseph could not forgive his father. After the old man died, Grandfather wrote to his brother once more, but never received an answer."

David and Aaron, the two remaining brothers, had "done well in America," a point they rarely left unmentioned in their infrequent letters home. Since David's death, his eldest son, Arthur, had been sending the annual greetings to the Thalstadt branch of the family on the High Holidays each fall. He always wrote for all the *Amerikaner:* his younger brother, Richard Bentheim, in New York; his sister, Laura Bentheim Bloom, in Cincinnati; and Cousin Ted, in Philadelphia, who was the son of the late Aaron Bentheim, although his name, curiously enough, was not Bentheim at all but Theodore Benton, Esq.

This autumn, for the very first time, there had been no holiday greetings from America for Rosh Hashonoh. But then, to everyone's surprise, a telegram had arrived from Paris: TOURING EUROPE STOP ARRIVING THALSTADT 10:07 SUNDAY FOR BRIEF STAY STOP ARTHUR RICHARD CELIA.

Now they were here, the *Amerikaner*, those unknown, hardly plausible relations from a distant land—smiling and nodding and speaking their formal, odd-sounding German. They were sitting in the living room sipping Grandfather's festive champagne as matter-of-factly as if they had dropped in from around the corner. It was all very strange and confusing.

"How did you find your accommodations, dear Celia?" Aunt Hanni asked Cousin Arthur's daughter.

It had been decided at once to put up the travelers at the new Park Hotel, not so much for its elegance and excellent service (there were hotels of equal distinction in Thalstadt) but because it was felt that the Park's ultramodern design, smooth-running elevators, and general air of cool, impersonal efficiency would make the Americans feel at home.

Celia pushed at her dark-rimmed glasses. She sat on the sofa, legs drawn up under her, seemingly quite at ease. Looking her cousin over from behind Grandfather's armchair, Eva was forced to admit that Celia was not really pretty, the way American girls were reputed to be; but with her trim figure, bobbed chestnut-brown hair, and the direct, faintly amused look in her eyes (gray as Stefan's), she looked exactly as one would have wished her to look.

"The Park is very up-to-date, Aunt Hanni," Celia said. "Quite a change from those medieval inns Richard chose for us on our trip from Paris! Take that quaint little *Gasthaus* in Freiburg, all nooks and *Fachwerk* gables and scoured stone floors, unspoiled by running hot water and central heating —the way Europe ought to remain forever, at least for jaded New York bachelors in search of their roots!"

Richard laughed back at his niece. He was, Eva decided, clearly the most fascinating of the three Americans. There was something vexingly familiar about his firm-chinned profile. Was it a certain resemblance to Hans Albers, the film star, who often portrayed tweedy bachelors with jauntily tilted cigarette holders and hairlines just beginning to recede? Perhaps, but it was more than that.

Richard looked up. "So you are my cousin Jonas' daughter," he said with a friendly nod and added in English, "How are you, Eva?"

"Fine, sankyoo." Even without the lisp, she wasn't doing too badly.

Richard smiled, and suddenly Eva knew where she had seen his tanned, smooth-shaven features before. Taller, more rugged, more worldly than her father, he nonetheless looked startlingly like him. Even his quick, bristly kiss on her cheek carried the familiar whiff of cigarette smoke.

They really *are* our cousins, Eva thought, believing it for the first time. In a way, it made everything even stranger.

There was roast goose in honor of the *Amerikaner*, and in honor of the goose everyone else stayed for dinner as well. The round dining table was spread with a tablecloth of faded ivory lace; it had, Grandfather quietly reflected, graced holiday tables in the Bentheim family since the days when he and his long-lost brothers were boys in a small Rhineland village.

It was a meal to be remembered long, as rich in family feeling and transatlantic goodwill as Anna's gravy was in texture and savor. At the head of the table, Eva's mother presided over the proceedings with flushed cheeks and flustered graciousness, noticeably comforted by Anna's unobtrusive assistance. Richard and Eva's father talked animatedly about American book publishing. Aunt Hanni, using her fine hands expressively, conversed in fluent English with the austere Cousin Arthur, managing at once to direct her words toward the little button in his ear and to appear utterly unaware of it. Stefan, having arrived unannounced from Heidelberg on his motorcycle, was seated next to Celia and held forth engagingly, if with a touch of condescension, on the merits of a European education. Grandfather complimented Anna on her cooking and wondered if another chilled bottle of champagne might be brought up from the cellar. Only Uncle Ludwig remained his taciturn self, disdaining to entertain or impress the *Amerikaner*. But Aunt Gustl, determined to carry the day for the Upstairs, had slyly maneuvered a seat between Grandfather and Cousin Arthur, from where she invited everyone in hearty Bavarian tones to partake of the fare.

It was Ella, however, for whom the dinner turned out to be most memorable of all. Seated at Richard's left, she was the object of his gravely courteous attention, which she returned with a modesty that was rare for her, voice low and eyes demurely lowered to her plate. From their traditional place at the foot of the table, Uschi and Eva observed her progress with envy and grudging admiration. All had gone well when, toward the end of the meal, Richard unexpectedly turned to Ella over the whipped cream meringue and addressed her in a few carefully spoken words in English. Uschi and Ella held their breaths, ready to bask in Ella's glory and concede once and for all her superiority in English and in all other matters.

But whether it was the sip of champagne Grandfather had allowed her or the disconcerting attractiveness of the

American cousin, Ella grew visibly alarmed. A deep blush rose to her face; she opened her mouth, stared at her mother with a look of despair in her usually stolid eyes, and dropped her fork, spattering cake crumbs and whipped cream over her sky-blue skirt.

Uschi and Eva ate their dessert in shocked silence, relieved that they were still safely anchored at the far end of the table, secure from the pleasures and pitfalls of the unpredictable adult world.

3 ✿✿✿

The following week, the family saw the travelers off on the next lap of their journey, to Italy. The *Amerikaner* had spent a few short, crowded days being whisked about Thalstadt and the surrounding countryside. They had admired the view of the city in autumnal sunlight from the Buchberg and had watched the sun go down, and the lights in the valley spring up, from the steep terrace of the Burg Café. They had been taken through Schloss Solitude and shown the famous curving desk of Karl der Dicke, and they had seen the industrial displays at the Technical Institute which, Richard readily conceded, compared with current U.S.A. design. They visited the Art Museum and the Dietz auto works on the Neckar; attended the season's opera premiere at the Staatstheater; and afterward, in the lamp-lit park, watched the white swans glide silently across the midnight waters of the pond. Now they felt, as they assured the Thalstadt Bentheims, that they had seen the best their city had to offer and would take lasting memories back home with them.

"And when will you bring the family to visit us in

America, Uncle Jakob?" Celia asked, smiling at Grandfather through her dark-rimmed glasses.

They sat on the covered verandah of the Schloss Café across from the railway station for last-minute refreshments to boost the Americans' flagging energies for the long journey south. The late afternoon sun, no longer warming but deceptively bright, cast a copper aura over Celia's hair. No wonder Grandfather smiled back at her.

He clipped off the tip of his cigar with his little scissors and shook his head. "America is a place for young people, my dear," he said comfortably. "I'm afraid I should be much too slow for your famous American tempo, too set in my ways to keep up with your fashions and fads, too clumsy, at my age, to struggle with those clever new gadgets of yours."

Richard held his streamlined lighter to Grandfather's cigar. "You do yourself an injustice, Sir," he said with that serious smile which seemed to Eva so much like her father's. "Permit me to add: you are not doing America justice, either. America isn't all tempo and things. We have our own traditions, perhaps a bit deeper beneath the surface than yours over here, but in the long run perhaps more dependable."

Across the table, Eva's father looked up with troubled eyes. He had not been feeling well these past weeks, and Eva had heard her mother complain to Aunt Hanni that the unceasing round of hospitalities had left him exhausted. Now the late sunlight traced deep lines in his finely boned face.

"To Father, this is the best of all possible worlds," he said. "I find myself praying at times, to that weary old family God of ours, that he shall never be disappointed."

He folded his hands around his coffee cup as if to seek warmth.

Uncle Ludwig smiled his skeptical smile. "As you see, Richard, my brother is an avid newspaper reader who makes the not uncommon mistake of believing what he reads. Newspapers are in the business of playing up the sensational: the ravings of a rabble-rouser from the Vienna slums, the scribblings of a few illiterate hatemongers no decent German would dream of taking seriously—"

"But millions of Germans are supporting Hitler's party," Richard interrupted with a trace of impatience. "Over a third of the voters in your last elections."

"And almost two-thirds did *not*," Uncle Ludwig said. "It all depends on how you look at it."

He shrugged and rested his eyes on Ella and Uschi, who were stirring their straws to jiggle the ice in their lemonade glasses.

"No, they have missed their chances, these gentlemen. The economy is improving, promising better days. Who knows, in a few years we might even take Celia up on her invitation and send our daughters for a semester or two at one of those girls' colleges of yours. Travel is broadening," he added, as if he felt called upon to justify his grandiose plans, for Uncle Ludwig was not a man given to boasting.

Celia's direct gray gaze was serious for once. "When I was a little girl, Grandfather David sometimes would talk to me about Germany, about his youth in the Rhineland. Now I find your country even more beautiful than I had imagined. Yet, somehow, it is a different country from the one he described for me. There seems to be so much bitterness beneath the courteous smiles, a sense of futility in people's eyes, as if they were no longer able to act for themselves, as if they were merely marking time for something to happen to them—anything, anyone."

She drew her traveling coat closer about her shoulders. "I keep thinking of what someone once said—a young instructor in my freshman year: that democracy is only skin-deep in Germany and that the people are still waiting for Barbarossa to ride forth from that mountain cave of his and lead them to some glorious destiny."

"Celia!" Cousin Arthur fumbled with the little button in his ear as if to shut out his daughter's voice. "That is the kind of thing you can expect from one of our better girls' colleges, Ludwig. Radical professors making pronouncements on things they know nothing about; young girls, sent off to school to learn how to be charming companions and gracious hostesses, returning home filled with a hodge-podge of wild socialistic theories! It's my guess, Celia, that Germany will always know how to maintain law and order far better than we at home with our anarchists and labor agitators!"

Eva's father lit a cigarette and absently doused the flame in a trickle of coffee in his saucer. "Law and order, like beauty, are in the eye of the beholder, Arthur. There seemed to be law and order in Italy last summer, when Martha and I vacationed there. But when I asked the headwaiter about Signor Carlo, who had been taking care of us in other seasons, he shook his head and quickly held his finger to his lips."

"What happened, Jonas?" Celia asked softly.

Eva exchanged a look of concern with her mother. Her father had always loved Italy—its healing southern climate, the brilliant colors of its countryside, its spirited people who were so different from his own somber nature and that of the stolid Swabian burghers. But when he had come back last year, after the elderly waiter's unexplained disappearance, he had told his doctors that he would never go there again, not while such dark and terrible things could happen in the bright Riviera sun. Even now, talking about it to Celia, his face looked transparently pale.

"What happened to Carlo, Celia? And to Dr. Galda, the Milanese book dealer who furnished me with some of the finest art volumes in Europe? My letters have been returned unclaimed, though Mussolini boasts that the Milan Express runs strictly on schedule these days."

Celia impulsively held out her hand. "You must leave Europe, Jonas. All of you must! I'm afraid for you here, afraid the day might come when my own letters might be returned unclaimed. Come to America! I know it will not be easy to leave your country for a land whose ways and culture are foreign to you. But remember that there are Bentheims in our country, too, ready to tide their Thalstadt cousins over to new beginnings."

"What kind of talk is this, Celia?" Arthur said sharply. "Have you lost all sense of proportion, yes, of propriety? The Thalstadt Bentheims have everything one could hope for here—an established business, a reputation in their community, a life of comfort and security. You want them to give up all this because of some unfounded, undefined fear of yours? At a time when the streets of New York are filled with the homeless and unemployed?"

"Arthur!" Richard said in a low, embarrassed voice.

Arthur doesn't *want* us to come, Eva thought, surprise and hurt giving way to relief. She wouldn't be "homeless in the streets of New York."

Into the sudden, awkward silence around the table,

Grandfather's cool voice slipped smoothly, soothingly, like mellow Rhineland wine. " 'Why wander to a distant land, when goodness lies so close at hand?' " He winked at Celia. "Do they teach Goethe at your American schools, my dear? A pity if they do not. I find him most appropriate in all kinds of situations. Yes, Goethe is a master at the art of living—equable, detached, serene. I sometimes rather wish we all could learn to regard life more philosophically. It wasn't Goethe, of course, who cautioned against throwing out the baby with the bath water, but it's a good German homily, nonetheless, even for young American ladies abroad."

He raised his glass in his firm old hand. "To many future visits of the *Amerikaner!*" His voice was steady and clear and tinged with a subtle irony. "They will always find Germany on the map—and the Bentheims in Germany!"

Ice tinkled in tall glasses and everyone laughed with sudden relief, as if a spell had been broken. An attentive waiter hurried over with a frosted jug of fresh lemonade. The unbidden shadows retreated; Grandfather had won the day. But even as she held out her glass, Celia's eyes swept over the others at the table, and suddenly she put her arm about Eva and drew her close.

A little while later, in the October dusk, the Thalstadt Bentheims stood on the station platform waving their handkerchiefs in the soot-filled air, while Celia and Richard leaned from the windows of the moving train and waved back, becoming smaller and smaller, until the speeding wheels carried them out of sight.

4 ⁂

The next day, when Eva came home from school for the midday meal, she thought for a moment that Richard had returned. A man's trench coat hung in the foyer, and there were company voices from the living room. But there was also the woody scent of a pipe, and Richard had smoked cigarettes.

"Visitors," Anna said as Eva came into the kitchen to peek into the steaming soup tureen. "Go wash up quickly. Everyone's waiting for you, as usual!"

Dinner guests at a moment's notice were no problem to Anna, who rose to such emergencies by adding some bouillon cubes to the broth, slicing the pot roast a little thinner, and running up to the attic for one more wax-sealed jar of her strawberry compote. Grandfather frequently brought unannounced diners: an out-of-town salesman lonesome for home-cooked food and conversation; or one of the store employees: Herr Sachs, the window-dresser, whose smooth High German always sounded faintly suspect to plain Swabian ears; Herr Emcke, the bookkeeper; or Viktor, the dashing salesman. No one terribly interesting, Eva concluded smugly, unwilling to recall that she had been secretly smitten with Viktor for two whole months when he first came to work for Bentheim & Sons. But Viktor, so darkly debonair on the familiar territory of the store, proved to be oddly reticent, yes, positively awkward at the dinner table; and when he opened his mouth at all, it was invariably to talk about his redhaired fiancée, who worked in the ladies' department at the shoestore on the square and rode in the sidecar of Viktor's motorcycle on Sunday afternoons.

Nevertheless, Eva decided she had better brush her hair before going in to dinner.

Her mother was already ladling out the soup, and her father was bringing the visitors to the table. They were Herr Valtary, the art dealer, and a strange boy.

Eva shook hands and sat down next to Grandfather, twisting her spoon to hide an obstinate ink spot on her thumb.

"You remember Herr Valtary, Eva?" her father said.

The wineglass next to his plate was still untouched, but his face seemed less pale and his voice sounded lighter. Her father was sentimental about things and people out of his past; and though they seemed to disagree on most subjects, he always enjoyed the art dealer's visits.

"Of course she remembers! Did we not drink champagne together on her grandfather's birthday in April?" Herr Valtary said in his suave manner. "I would like Eva to meet my nephew, though. But I think it only fair to warn her: Arno takes after his uncle in his appreciation of pretty girls."

Herr Valtary laughed inordinately at his joke, and the boy looked up, unimpressed. "Pleased to meet you," he said stiffly.

He sat very straight, his lanky shoulders squared. His dark, stubbornly wavy hair was cut very short and his brows merged in a dusky streak of down above dark eyes and a too delicately modeled nose. His mouth seemed oddly vulnerable, almost defenseless.

She caught her mother's meaningful look: she had been staring again!

"Pleased to meet you, Arno," she mumbled hastily and painfully swallowed a spoonful of stinging hot soup.

She had not brought it off nearly as smoothly as Arno had. But it did not matter. She had already decided not to like him.

After dinner, while Grandfather napped in his armchair by the window, her father and his guest talked over brandies.

Herr Valtary tilted his chair so far it seemed he would topple over backwards. One of his legs rested on the piano bench, the other supported the perilous tilt of his chair. Thick clouds of pipe smoke rose toward the ceiling.

"You are a dreamer, Bentheim," he said with a short laugh. "You've been a dreamer ever since our days back at the Gymnasium. That's why I've always liked you! But you must really leave the fate of Germany to the men of action. Your parliamentarians have had their say for fourteen years, and look where they have brought us!"

Eva's father shrugged. "We are still new at governing ourselves in a democracy, Valtary. But you are ready to call in your man on horseback to cure all our ills with one stroke of the sword. Germany has had her fill of horse cures, Valtary. She needs wise, patient physicians to bind her wounds and nurse her back to health."

Herr Valtary smiled. "Why is it Jews are either the most practical of men or the most incorrigibly romantic? You're putting your cart before my horse, Bentheim. Let the strong men get Germany back on her feet, put an end to the blunderings of the Weimar socialists and democrats! And if von Papen has to make common cause with the devil himself to get the unemployed off the streets and restore order, I say: bring on the devil! We can always send him packing again once things are back in hand."

Eva's father shook his head. "Demons, as Goethe's apprentice sorcerer found out to his grief, are not so easily dismissed once they are summoned. You call them in as humble water-bearers to do your dirty work, and they end up in the saddle, unloosing the floodgates of hell. No, it is neither 'practical' nor 'romantic' to make pacts with the devil, Valtary: the collateral is too high. If you get your soul back at all, chances are it will have suffered permanent damage."

Eva's mother set a bowl of fruit on the table. "Why don't you take Arno to your room and show him your books and games, Eva," she said, with a smile for Herr Valtary. Her mother always treated the art dealer with particular courtesy, almost as if by her graciousness she might silently persuade him to spare her husband the strain of these turbulent discussions.

Eva pushed back her chair. She was less than eager to spend time with this strange and uncommunicative boy —and showing him her room, with her books and keepsakes lining the shelves, would be like telling him things about herself he could not care less to know. But there was something about the brightness of her mother's smile that was quite final. "Children mustn't be around when grown-ups speak about such matters," she often said. And this conversation about Chancellor von Papen and the Sorcerer's Apprentice (a poem that had seemed innocent enough when Frau Ackermann read it aloud in class but that suddenly, under her father's quiet words, took on some hidden, ominous meaning) was clearly one of "such matters."

Arno sat down on the window bench and Eva sat on the edge of her bed. He stuck his hands into his pockets, stretched his legs, and studied the shining tips of his shoes as if they bore an intricate design. After a while she realized that he was simply going to sit there, without saying a thing. She, the hostess, as her mother would say, would have to speak first.

"Do you live in Thalstadt, Arnold?" she began awkwardly. It seemed the kind of opening grown-ups would use when they were "making conversation."

"No, I'm just visiting. And my name is Arno. You see, I was born in Florence," he added.

"Oh," she said, puzzled.

For the first time, he looked up from his shoes, looked directly at her. "Florence, Italy. The Arno River." He smiled—a very nice smile, to her surprise. It was not a smile that said, as Ella would have: "Don't tell me you were absent from geography that day!"

She nodded. "You are Italian, then?" That explained it: the dark hair and smooth olive skin, that faintly foreign look about his finely etched features, different from the round-faced Thalstadt children she knew, as she herself had always been different.

He shook his head. "No, but my father travels to Italy a

lot; and when I was small, my parents lived in Florence for a time." He drew up his legs and hugged his knees. "You see, my father is an artist."

He said it slowly, almost solemnly, as if he were saying: my father is a king.

Suddenly everything fell into place for Eva. "Your father is Alex Valtary, the painter who did my grandfather's portrait!"

She would have liked to tell him of her secret about Grandfather—how she had discovered it again in his father's painting. But she could not.

"Would you like to see the picture?" she asked instead. "It hangs in the drawing room. Everyone who comes to the house goes to see it."

"I did see it, before you got home from school," Arno said. "Your grandfather looks a little older now, but I think my father would paint him the same way again."

"To flatter him?" Eva laughed.

"No, to tell the truth. Your grandfather hasn't given *in* to time. I don't imagine he ever will. My father paints people as they *are*, not as they seem to others."

Her mother came in, carrying Eva's music sheets. "It's time for your piano lesson, Eva. Perhaps Arno would like to walk you part of the way?"

Eva bit her lip. How like her mother to get her into embarrassing situations! Like the time she had made her play Liszt's "Liebestraum" for her sewing-circle ladies when they would clearly have preferred giving their undivided attention to their pastries and conversation. Now she had done it again! Arno, to be sure, got up at once and remained standing stiffly and correctly until her mother had left the room.

Eva went to the closet and pulled her coat off the hanger. "You don't *have* to, you know," she said, as coolly as she could. "I always walk by myself. It gives me time to *think*."

To her surprise, her heart was beating sharply. Now if he wouldn't come, she could at least pretend it did not matter.

Arno followed her into the hall and held the apartment door for her. She started down the stairs, not daring to look back. After a long moment she heard the door close and the sound of his steps on the stairs, first slowly, then two at a time, until he caught up with her in the lobby.

The October day had faded into a gray mist. Arno took her music and walked beside her in his customary silence. She wondered if her mother had remembered to give her the book with her Mozart Sonata that Fräulein Lehmann had promised to start her on. But she decided not to turn back in any case. She could always work on the other pieces: next time her mother inflicted her on her long-suffering ladies, she might even bring off a fairly tolerable "Liebestraum."

The thought struck her so funny, suddenly, that she could hardly keep from laughing out loud.

Arno looked at her sideways. "What do you think about when you go for walks by yourself?"

"Hm?" One had to weigh one's words carefully with this strange, quiet boy. He had a knack of remembering what one said, and taking it seriously, too.

"Oh—nothing much," she said, wishing he'd not persist. She would rather die than tell him she sometimes made up poems in her head. What boy would have anything further to do with a girl who admitted to things of that sort?

He nodded gravely, as if he understood very well. "You think about your music. But that is nothing to hide. I do the same, only I must think about it at night, just before going to sleep. You see, you are lucky to have those walks by yourself. I am never alone during the day."

She felt happy all of a sudden, without knowing why. Perhaps it was merely walking next to Arno, watching him unobserved, the way his downy eyebrows met above his fine nose and eyes. Or perhaps it was that she suddenly knew it would not matter about those poems; not with Arno.

"You play the piano, too, Arno—no, it's the violin!" she guessed wildly, picturing him on the stage of the Thalstadt Conservatory, grave and pale and darkly handsome, taking his bow under a burst of applause. "And you're never alone because you have a houseful of brothers and sisters. They all play instruments and sing and your mother plays the piano and your father sticks his head out of his studio and begs everyone to stop so he can finish his painting in time for the Munich Art Exhibit!"

The sun, with that unpredictability of late October, lit up the corners of the Thalstadt sky.

Arno shifted the music sheets to his free arm. "Yes, I play the violin," he said.

Not a word more. She wondered what she had said to make him withdraw from her again, but she did not dare ask. She had spoiled everything; that much was clear.

"*Auf Wiedersehen*, Arno," she said at the door to Fräulein Lehmann's house. And added, stiffly, the way adults ended their silly conversations, "I enjoyed making your acquaintance."

He handed her the music sheets. "I live at boarding school, outside Munich. When my mother died, my father started to travel a lot again because of his work; so sometimes during vacation, I stay with Uncle Hans. I'll see you again, next time I am in Thalstadt—in the spring."

5 ⁂

Suddenly it was winter.

One morning Eva found her window spattered with a fine white spray: twined tendrils of frozen blossoms that caught the fading glow of the November sun and set it ablaze in the glass. She leaned her forehead against the pane and watched her breath dissolve the crystal swirls into thin rivulets that weakly ran down the glass. With the tip of her finger she drew a circle on the misted pane, with dots for eyes and an upturned curve for the mouth, and then another circle, with the mouth curving *down*. She stood back: the two faces were exactly alike except that one looked happy, the other sad—as she herself would often be happy one moment and sad the next. " 'High as the sky or sad unto death,' " Anna would say, shaking her head.

Eva sighed and carefully drew a third circle on the glass, keeping the mouth perfectly straight.

Outside, under a light brushstroke of snow, the *Gässle* was silent, as if the old houses were hibernating behind their drawn shutters. Across the street, in the attic window of the Muenzer house, the Muenzers' boarder, Frau Dorn, raised her wrinkled round face and peered nearsightedly from eyes at once bright and blank, like those of the vagrant sparrows on her window ledge. She sprinkled a handful of seeds into the frosty air and watched the whir of wings flutter up like a cloud and swoop to the cobblestones below. Huddled into her gray shawl, she leaned over the window-sill and waved her hands, a blustering sparrow flapping its wings. . . .

Eva's mother took the winter clothes out of the closet.

Standing in front of her mother's tall dresser mirror, Eva was made to try on her last year's things one by one, while Fräulein Hubmaier, the seamstress, knelt at her feet and touched the hems against her knees.

"This one might do for one more season, Frau Bentheim," Fräulein Hubmaier murmured tactfully through a mouthful of pins, while Eva stared over her head out the window. She *hadn't* "shot up" over the summer, as Fräulein Hubmaier had cheerfully predicted on her spring visit, and she was determined to give not the slightest hint that she either remembered or cared.

Fräulein Hubmaier was pretty, plump, and possessed of a formidable bosom, which, bent over the sewing machine, displayed itself to full advantage in a succession of low-cut, ingeniously draped blouses of various pastel shades. Every autumn and spring she set up shop for a few cluttered days in a corner of the foyer, proceeding to transform Frau Bentheim's last-year's styles into "the latest from Paris," sheathing sofa pillows in artfully pleated satins of brilliant hues, and putting "false hems" on favorite old tweed skirts that even Eva had managed to outgrow. Frequently, too, Fräulein Hubmaier was enlisted to rescue some hapless garment or smock that Eva had designed in sewing class and set out to make with a great spurt of good intentions, but which, by the end of the school year, wrinkled, sticky and limp, hung in her closet unfinished, a mute, insistent reproach.

"What do you think, Frau Bentheim?" Fräulein Hubmaier asked appraisingly, holding the hem of last year's winter coat flat against Eva's legs, a safe quarter inch below the top of her knee socks. It was a coat of gray-blue wool, with a little gray collar and cuffs of tightly curled fur, and it smelled of mothballs and the winter before: of bright, windless Sunday mornings when she and Uschi had fed peanuts to the tame, rust-colored squirrels in the park; lamp-lit late afternoons, and the walk home from piano lessons through a light swirl of snow; wet, bristling days, when she and Renate would run all the way from school to the streetcar stop to keep their toes from freezing even in the heavy socks with brightly striped borders so painstakingly fashioned in Fräulein Kugler's knitting class. Eva had forgotten, over the long warm season and leisurely fall; her winter memories, too, had been securely stashed away in some well-sealed and secret place and now came out of their wraps, surprisingly whole, naphtha-scented and smooth and warm, like the feel of the gray fur cuffs against her fingertips.

She turned before the mirror, observing the flare of the blue hem. "Looks fine," she said airily, clutching the fur collar against her throat in a grand-lady gesture that was indubitably Sabine.

"I met Frau Rubin on Koenigstrasse this afternoon, Eva,"

her mother said over supper. "She and Thea would like you to come for Friday evening dinner. If you decide to go, Thea will pick you up."

If she decided to go! She and Thea had been friends all their lives, seeing each other every week—at Hebrew lessons, at Fräulein Lehmann's piano classes, and as often as possible at other times. Though not as often as Eva would have liked, for there were now three younger children in Thea's family, and her mother needed Thea's help.

"Thea takes on so much responsibility at home," Eva's mother would say approvingly. But there was that faint note of implied reproach for Eva's own *ir*responsible ways which made her angry not merely at her mother but, at such moments, even at Thea herself. That their friendship survived these unspoken comparisons, and that Thea remained totally unaware of them, was perhaps the most amazing thing about her.

But then, Thea never ceased to amaze Eva. She was, despite a surface impression of calm, an intense and strong-willed girl. Her blue eyes shone; her face with its square chin and wide, Tartar cheekbones, was perhaps less than pretty; but in its vividness and strength, it was almost beautiful. Next to Thea, Eva thought herself a drab and spineless creature, and her pride in being Thea's friend was always tempered by the apprehension that, someday, Thea might become aware of Eva's unworthiness and find someone better.

The Rubins lived on the fourth floor of an apartment building on Verastrasse. Approached from the street, Thea's house seemed like any other city dwelling. But on Eva's first visit, she discovered to her surprise a grassy backyard with stunted city trees climbing a steep earthen slope. In the scant shade of these gnarled, uncared-for trees, Thea and Eva often sat on summer afternoons, talking away the slow, humming hours while the younger children played nearby. It was only to Thea, and only in this secret place of theirs, that Eva could speak about some things: hurtful things, like not being thought pretty; scary, marvelous things, like wanting to write poems and stories someday, good enough to be printed in books. And Thea would understand and talk about being a pioneer on a settlement in Palestine—Eretz Yisrael, she would say—like her cousin Michael, whose picture she kept on her dresser: a tanned, stocky young man in work clothes and visored cap, standing in a vast, sun-flooded landscape barren of trees. It seemed a stark and desolate place compared to the green hills of Swabia. But whenever Eva asked Thea why she wanted to live there, she would say simply, "To build a homeland for all Jews."

Occasionally, after piano lessons, Thea would come back to Eva's house, and they would sit down on the black piano bench and go over their "four-handed" pieces together. Thea, Fräulein Lehmann's honor pupil, played the difficult bass part and kept the count for them both. Sometimes Thea could even stay for supper, but only if there was no meat on the Bentheim table that evening; the Rubins were observing Jews who strictly kept the dietary laws, the Sabbath rest, and all the holidays.

And yet, though Eva's parents were fond of Thea and on the most cordial terms with the Rubins, a remoteness remained between the two families, as if they were separated by a thin glass wall through which one could smile and talk and gesture, but never quite reach hands. It puzzled and disturbed Eva, yet for some reason not entirely clear to her, she never dared raise the question with Thea.

Nor did Eva ask her mother. That Herr Rubin worked in a factory and Thea's mother ran her busy household without outside help could have nothing to do with the matter: with some people such things might count, but Eva's parents, happily, were not among them. Nor would it matter to them that the Rubins were "religious" while the Bentheims were "liberal." Eva's grandparents in Ettingen did not mix meat and milk, nor did Aunt Tilla, Uncle Lutz's wife; and the divergence in family customs and views led to nothing more serious than an occasional quip and endless, inconclusive family debates.

Finally, it was Thea herself who supplied the cue.

In winter, on the way home from Hebrew lessons in the musty schoolroom behind the synagogue, Eva sometimes succeeded in coaxing Thea to come home with her for an hour's play. After Anna had thawed them out with cups of hot cocoa at the kitchen table, they rummaged through the big closet in the foyer for ruffled ladies' dresses long out of style, the Japanese parasol Eva's father had won at a New Year's Eve raffle, the beaded evening bag and fringed golden theater shawl Eva dimly remembered seeing her mother wear to the opera back in the days when Eva had still been very young.

Sometimes, in this unlikely finery, they would act out the Bible stories the cantor had taught them in class that afternoon. Then Eva was Deborah, brave leader and judge in Israel, and Thea was Miriam, sister of Moses, singing her freedom psalm to the rhythm of two pot lids borrowed from Anna in place of the ancient cymbals.

Caught in the spell of their game one winter afternoon, they paid no attention to the doorbell. But after a moment

Anna came into the room, rubbing her hands in consternation.

"Someone's at the door, Eva," she said, "an old man with a funny hat and the queerest clothes—and I can't make out a word he is saying."

A glimmer of recognition flickered in Thea's blue eyes, but Eva barely noticed. Peddlers and wandering journeymen in search of work often came to the door in these bitter times; but an old man in strange clothes who couldn't make himself understood by Anna?

"Come on, Thea, let's see!" Eva cried and ran out into the hall, tripping over her costume in her haste.

An old man, bearded and gaunt, stood in the doorway. His head was covered with a wide-brimmed black hat, and from his stooped shoulders hung a black cloak that barely skimmed the dusty tips of his shoes.

Eva stared at him with an awe close to fear. But, unwilling to let Thea guess her uneasiness, she hid her flushed face in the trailing sleeve of her kimono and giggled sheepishly.

Thea gently pushed her aside. She went up to the stranger and put her hand into his pale, hesitant one. They spoke, but Eva could not understand what they were saying, though here and there a phrase sounded hauntingly reminiscent—of German and some other language, too. Was it Hebrew?

The old man raised his arms and let them drop in a gesture of resignation. "A *shtickl brott*," he murmured.

Eva felt the blood rush to her face. *Brott—Brot—*He was asking for *bread*, and she had laughed at him!

"Could you give him something to eat, Anna?" Thea asked quietly. "Some bread and warm tea is all he would accept. And let him rest in your kitchen for a while? He has lost his way and still has far to go before dark."

For the briefest of moments, Anna hesitated, glancing from her gleaming oaken floors to the dusty, caked shoes of the stranger.

Then she gingerly put her hand on his black sleeve. "Mother of God, I wouldn't turn a tired old man away from my kitchen, would I, Thea?" she said, holding the door ajar.

"But how did you know how to speak to him, Thea?" Eva asked later as they were putting away their costumes in silence, oddly ashamed of their childish games.

"I've heard my parents speak in his language, Eva," Thea said. "The old man comes from Poland, where Jews still speak his ancient Yiddish tongue." She handed Eva the two pot lids, which no longer were cymbals. "You see, my parents were born in Poland. They are strangers, too."

6 🌲🌲🌲

A sharp November wind whistled across the square when
Thea called for Eva on Friday afternoon. From the bleak
sky a few snowflakes drifted tentatively, as if the cold had
scared them away. Thea knotted her kerchief tighter
around her crisp blond hair; Eva noticed that the sleeves of
her last year's coat had grown short: between cuffs and
mittens, Thea's wrists were reddened by the winter cold.

They hurried along the twilight streets with their arms
about each other, huddling close to the walls of the houses.

"Let's stop at the bakery for a minute, Thea," Eva
suggested. "Their pretzels are fresh out of the oven at this
hour, and we could warm up a little inside the store."

Thea shook her head. "I ought to get home before
sundown, Eva, before Mother lights the Sabbath candles.
Besides," she added with a smile, "we don't want to spend
our money on pretzels this time of year. We'll soon have to
buy Hanukkah presents."

Eva hung back. The promise of warmth and the aroma of
the fresh pretzels tempted her to break an unspoken
agreement between them and offer to pay for Thea's
purchase. But as if she had guessed Eva's thoughts and

wanted to spare her the humiliation of a refusal, Thea quickened her pace until they were safely beyond the bright lights of the bakery.

"Let's take the short-cut up the steps, Eva," Thea said at the corner of Hohe Strasse. "The Nazis are holding another rally up the street, pushing their leaflets and swastika badges. I could hardly get past them on the way down."

Thalstadt children were used to running up the many flights of steps around their hill-ringed city, even when the steps were slick underfoot with hardening snow, as they were on this late afternoon. Thea and Eva were half way to the top before they slowed down to catch their breath. Between the rooftops they caught a glimpse of Hohe Strasse below—a dark knot of people around a speaker whose swastika-banded arm was flailing the air with the short, choppy motions of a wind-up doll; Eva half-expected to see a key protruding from the back of his coat. From where they stood leaning over the railing, he did not look especially menacing; if anything, he looked ridiculous, even pathetic. Except for the tight wall of brown uniforms and heavy boots around him. And for the fragments of slogans the wind carried across the rooftops. . . "international Jewish Bolsheviks . . . parasitic Jewish capitalists . . ."

"You're shivering, Eva," Thea said. "Come on, Mother will get some hot soup into you as soon as my father comes home from work."

"I think I know that man, Thea," Eva said slowly, leaning over the railing to get a better look at the face of the speaker under the down-turned brim of his hat. "His name is Georg."

She could not bring herself to tell the rest, not even to Thea. How would she manage to tell her mother? And

Fräulein Brenner—did she know? Did she approve? Or would she still say that men come and go, Frau Bentheim, but one's good name . . .

Thea was pulling at her sleeve. "You couldn't recognize Hitler himself from this distance, Eva," she said with a laugh. "So whoever it is you think you're seeing, I wouldn't be too sure."

"I guess you're right," Eva said, after a final look across the railing, and followed Thea up the steps. Of course she could not be sure—there had been other occasions when she had "let her imagination run away with her," as her father would point out to her with a shake of his head. The real Georg, on second thought, had been a bit taller, smoother—quite different, actually, except for that down-turned hat. It was the hat that had fooled her, she thought with a surge of relief; she would not have to tell her mother anything. There was nothing to tell.

By the time they had reached the top of the stairs, the rally on Hohe Strasse was breaking up and the speaker had melted into the crowd.

Miriam opened the door for them, reaching up to kiss her sister as if she had been gone for a week. Martin, doing his homework at the kitchen table, looked up from his book and waved.

Frau Rubin was setting the Sabbath table.

"I'm so glad you could come, Eva," she called out from the living room. Her precise High German was etched with the merest trace of a foreign accent and her dark eyes in the pale, elegant face were tinged with a lingering sadness, as if they had seen and remembered much.

"Sit down, Mother. Eva and I will finish the table," Thea said.

Frau Rubin sighed and walked to the window. It was almost dark outside and snow whirled in the headlights of the passing cars. She gazed into the winter dusk while the girls washed up and bustled about the table, placing the silver candlesticks in the center.

"There is your father, Thea!" Frau Rubin called out at last and quickly untied her apron. "Now we can begin."

A key turned at the end of the long hall, and a few minutes later Thea's father came into the room with a quiet greeting. Snow glistened on his crisp, close-cropped hair, which was blond like Thea's but faded and shot with gray. He held his hands over the warm tiles of the oven and stamped his feet. Then he drew up his chair and heavily sat down at the table.

His wife placed the cloth-covered Sabbath bread before him for the blessing.

"And what did Herter say?" she asked, picking up the thread of a conversation nobody else had heard.

He shrugged. "Two more weeks, perhaps three. After that the machines will stand idle till spring."

"Perhaps some orders will come in before then," his wife said, her hand on his bowed shoulder.

"And if there are no orders, Leah? The children—"

"The children will eat, Abner," she said quietly. "Was it for Solomon's riches our parents brought us here when *we* were young? To be safe and together, with no one to break down our door and call our children names in the street —isn't that *dayenu?*"

He reached for her hand. "Enough, if it's God's will —*dayenu.*"

Miriam ran from the kitchen into her father's out-stretched arms—a slight girl with her mother's dark hair and eyes. Martin closed his book and went to bring the baby from his crib.

"Sit down, Eva—there, between Thea and myself," Thea's father said, pouring the dark red wine into the silver-ornamented *kiddush* cup.

His wife lit the tall white candles. The light flickered and flared, casting its glow over her motionless hands, her face in repose. For a moment, her hands remained suspended over the flames; then she let them drop away, let them glide over her forehead as if to push away the care of the workaday world.

"*Gut Shabbes, Kinderle!*" she said, smiling at her husband over the cup he held out to her. "A very good Sabbath to all."

7 ☘☘☘

For her birthday on the eighth of December, Inge Beisswanger invited the entire class.

"It's so much simpler," she said with a shrug. They were in the girls' locker room after gym period. "Now Mother won't have to bother sending out invitations."

She clambered on top of the big metal chest which held the gym supplies. "*Everyone come to my paaaaarty!*" she called through her cupped hands. Her hair clung to her damp forehead in tight blond ringlets. Her snugly fitting gymsuit cut grooves into her chubby shoulders.

"Are the boys invited?" Renate asked, bending over her knee to slip off her gym shoes.

"Yes, your beloved Horst will be there!" Inge cried and jumped off the chest with a loud thud. "But I've already told Mother he is to sit next to *me!*"

"Stop it, Inge. I don't *like* Horst, I've told you!" Renate said, her pert upper lip trembling dangerously. "Horst is cruel."

"Well, if you don't like my friends, Renate, you needn't come to my party," Inge said snappishly, slipping her skirt over her head and cinching her full waist with a wide red belt. She ran a comb through her tangled curls and gazed at her flushed face in the locker mirror. What she saw seemed to please her immensely.

"Of course, you must come, Renate. I was only joking!" She pulled Renate's pigtail as a gesture of reconciliation and giggled. "I may even ask Mother to let you sit on Horst's *other* side."

The Beisswanger villa was on The Heights, not far from the walled estate of Herr Hallenbeck.

Renate was waiting for Eva at the last trolley stop. The streetcar line ended a fair distance below Inge's house, and perhaps because of this, she arrived at school each morning in the family Mercedes driven by a smartly uniformed chauffeur.

"Just the same, her mother ought to make her walk," Renate said, trudging ahead. "It might do her some good."

Renate was still sulking over Inge's teasing, and overhead, the swollen sky seemed to sulk along with her. The drizzle of rain that had hung over the city since early morning had turned heavier, and their galoshes squeaked drearily over the steep, slushy path. In summer it would have been lovely to walk uphill under the full-leafed trees; now the gnarled branches were bare and the rain fell between them, desolately, relentlessly.

In the quiet, in the rain, it seemed easier to ask Renate something Eva had often wanted to ask her before.

"About Horst, Renate. Do you really like him, as Inge said?" She looked away quickly, afraid of what Renate might answer.

Renate ducked her head under a low-hanging branch. A shower of droplets sprayed over her blue kerchief.

"Sometimes I think I do, Eva, but I wish I didn't," she

said in a small voice. "And then again, I really don't, but I wish he were different and I could. . . ." She looked up anxiously. "Do you know what I mean, Eva?"

Eva nodded halfheartedly. What Renate had said was confusing, but there was something about the troubled look in her eyes that almost made Eva understand.

Besides, one word too many and Renate might burst into tears. Tears came as easily to Renate as laughter came to most children. If she could not come up with an answer in class, if she found herself standing on the field with the other "leftovers" when everyone else had been chosen for the *Völkerball* teams, or if she discovered that she had left her history notebook at home, the treacherous tears would well up in her eyes and roll down her flat-cheeked face in large, childish drops.

But Renate cried hardest whenever Horst taunted her; unlike the other girls, she seemed unable to regard his dubious attentions as a mark of distinction. Yet though she never joined in applauding Horst's victories on the ballfield, it was Renate who unaccountably one afternoon had dabbed Horst's scraped and bleeding knee with her handkerchief after a particularly ferocious game. "Renate loves Horst, Renate loves Horst!" the boys had howled as Horst, swaggering despite his limp, went back on the field for the final round, Renate's blood-soaked handkerchief around his knee. The girls cheered shrilly, and Horst, smiling his lazy, insolent smile, veered unexpectedly and struck Anton's chest with a glancing shot that left the frail boy gasping for breath. "For you, Renate!" Horst cried mockingly, but Renate had turned away and walked from the sunny, swarming field, the tears welling helplessly in her eyes.

"And what about Anton, Renate?" Eva asked after a while, through the rain falling in gray sheets between them. "I always thought you liked *Anton.*"

Renate looked at her in astonishment. "Of course I like Anton, Eva. We must like *everybody*, as Jesus loves all of us. To Jesus *everyone* is dear, and through Him everyone can go to heaven—even Horst. You, too, Eva," she added with sudden urgency, "if you could only learn to believe in Him."

Renate, a pastor's daughter brought up as devoutly in her Lutheran faith as Thea was in her Jewish one, had dropped such hints before. Each time Eva had tried to explain that, being Jewish, she had been taught to believe in God's love and mercy alone. But Renate would shake her head and repeat, eyes brimming, that Eva could get into heaven only if she believed in Jesus.

"If Horst goes to heaven, Renate, I'd rather go someplace else," Eva said now, trying to make light of it. Far enough away from Horst, she thought, so he could never again call her Little Jap, or brag about the island of Rügen, where only "real" Germans were allowed—not Jews like she. But Jesus had been Jewish too—King of the Jews, the Romans had mocked him. . . .

"Renate, would Jesus be allowed on Rügen?" she wondered out loud. But Renate, fretting about being late, was hurrying on ahead.

In the Beisswanger hall, a maid in a black dress and a frilly white apron and cap took their dripping coats. From somewhere above their heads, laughter and children's voices drifted down to them.

"We *are* late, Eva," Renate whispered uncomfortably.

They hurried up the flight of winding stairs, glad that the red carpet muffled their steps. On the landing, Inge's mother, an ample lady with pink and white skin powdered even whiter and pinker, extended a soft white hand. Her hair, profusely blond, was stylishly waved, and a lush lavender scent clung to her well-tailored curves.

"A pity you did not arrive just a bit sooner, girls," she said, choosing her words in that strained and stilted High German vainly meant to disguise the broad Thalstadt Swabian. "Wenzel, our chauffeur, made several runs to the streetcar stop and brought back all your classmates in the Mercedes."

"There are the stray lambs!" Inge cried, bursting through one of the doors.

Over her shoulder, Eva and Renate caught a bewildering glimpse of Inge's room, milling with birthday guests: her dresser, desk, and the ruffled pink spread on her bed piled high with brightly wrapped and ribboned boxes. Holding their own wilted packages numbly in wind-chilled hands, Renate and Eva exchanged a look of shared misery. Struggling uphill through the rain had been far less an ordeal than this conspicuous belated entrance amid the Beisswanger splendor.

But they went quite unnoticed. They had barely slipped into Inge's room and gingerly put their bedraggled offerings on a distant corner of the ruffled spread when the door opened once more and the maid announced with a smile that Fräulein Inge might bring her company to the table at any time. Frau Beisswanger was ready to cut the cake!

The heavy oaken table beneath the crystal chandelier ran

almost the full length of the dining room. Even so, Eva wondered how twenty-six children could be made to fit around it. But Frau Beisswanger strode ahead of them in her tight-fitting pumps with the confidence of the well-fed and well-corseted.

"You won't mind sitting next to our birthday child, Horst? And you, Monika—at Horst's left? And Klaus over there? and Diete?"

Evidently Inge had forgotten her promise to Renate. Or perhaps for some inscrutable grown-up reason, Frau Beisswanger had refused to go along with it.

But at the head of the table, Horst had eyes neither for Inge on his right nor Monika on his left. He stared at the door, through which a tea cart was slowly rolling across the red carpet, expertly guided by the smiling maid. In the center of the tea-cart tray was the birthday cake, a lavish pink and white affair piled high with whipped cream and decorated with a three-ring circus of candy animals and clowns.

Inge clapped her pudgy hands, her hair curling in damp ringlets about her flushed cheeks. "Marzipan piggies—my favorite, Mama!"

Frau Beisswanger, cutting the cake, smiled indulgently. Her fingers daintily wielded a slender ivory-handled knife. Golden bracelets jangled at her wrist.

"Would you believe it, children, this lovely knife came all the way from Africa! Grandfather Beisswanger often traveled there on business—in the old days, before the English took away our colonies." She sighed and discreetly licked a finger.

Then she picked up the ivory cake server and ceremoniously placed the first piece on Inge's plate. Horst was next—and held out his plate for a second helping before Frau Beisswanger had come full circle around the table.

When they had had their fill of birthday cake, Frau Beisswanger reached for the small silver bell next to her cup and rang.

"*Ach bitte*, Mariechen, would you bring in the trays with the cream puffs, éclairs, and *Schillerlocken?* We are about to have a contest. Whoever eats the most cake wins a birthday prize!"

Once again the tea cart rolled across the carpet, laden with pastries this time: a bakery window on wheels, Eva thought, like the one she and Thea had passed that bitter cold afternoon a few weeks before when Thea would not step inside to let her buy warm pretzels for them both. It seemed traitorous, all of a sudden, to eat the flaky *Schillerlocke* that Inge's mother eased onto her plate; it was almost as if by partaking of the Beisswangers' bounteous fare, they silently conspired to forget that others went without.

But would it not be ungrateful to offend Frau Beisswanger by refusing? Eva's scruples melted with the whipped cream on her tongue. Besides, there was the contest, and the exciting, flush-faced fellowship of it all! The room was hushed; only the forks scraped, the pastry crackled, and the cocoa spoons clinked. And Frau Beisswanger watched benignly over everything, keeping count of the helpings, coaxing little Helga Boehm into another try, admonishing Klaus not to cheat. Eva almost forgot that she had ever thought her foolish and ostentatious.

To everyone's surprise, Monika von Ahlem shook her head after the very first piece.

"*Nein, danke*, Frau Beisswanger, I *couldn't!*"

"*Ach*, Monika, you wouldn't spoil our little game!" Frau Beisswanger was genuinely puzzled, even hurt. "Children love contests. Don't *you?*"

"Not *that* kind," Monika said cryptically. She shrugged her pale hair back over her shoulder and shook her head languidly, as some ancestral noble lady might have refused the homage of a minor knight.

The cake server that had threatened to descend on Monika's plate paused in Frau Beisswanger's hand, wavered, and withdrew like a medieval battering ram before an unbreachable fortress. Frau Beisswanger had surrendered.

"Ready for my fourth, Mama!" Inge cried.

She and Horst were way ahead, though Klaus Herzog valiantly strove to catch up. The maid came in unobtrusively to switch on the crystal chandelier and draw the heavy drapes: the rain had grown into a dark torrent pelting the villa walls, but inside, behind the red velvet hangings, the room was bright and fragrant and safe.

Frau Beisswanger, shaking her head in mock vexation, was slipping a fifth helping onto Horst Reuter's plate.

"Why, Mama, look at Anton!" Inge suddenly cried through her custard éclair. "Anton isn't *eating!*"

Indeed, to everyone's disbelief, a drooping slice of birthday cake lay barely touched on Anton's plate. He sat stiffly behind it, holding his fork in his hand, his napkin—a cunning bit of camouflage—tucked under his starched white collar. Napkin and poised fork had evidently accomplished their intended mission: they had deceived Frau Beisswanger, and everyone else, concerning Anton's refusal to join in the game. Or had it gone unnoticed simply because Anton was seated at some forgotten corner of the table, left out of things at parties as easily as he was in class?

Frau Beisswanger drew her hand across her forehead. The endless cutting of cakes and filling of plates had wearied her.

"Anton? Oh, yes," she murmured uncertainly. Her face brightened. "Of course, the clever little fellow from the *Volksschule!* Inge has told me all about you, Anton!"

She crossed the room quickly, swaying a little on her tight pumps. "But surely *you* ought to enjoy this treat, Anton!" she said lightly, putting her white hand over Anton's and prodding his fork toward the porcelain plate.

"*Nein danke*, Frau Beisswanger," Anton said in a tight voice, cringing under the two rows of curious eyes that suddenly fastened on him.

"Your mother's cake isn't good enough for him, Inge," Horst Reuter said in a loud whisper. "He's used to better from the soup kitchen."

Frau Beisswanger pursed her lips. She released Anton's hand and pushed away his plate. "Well, perhaps Anton's taste runs to different things," she said cheerfully, but with an edge of steel to her voice.

She picked up one of the round trays and held it under Anton's flustered face—the cream puffs, éclairs, and *Schillerlocken* somewhat depleted now, but still delectable and inviting.

"Surely there is *something* here to tempt you, Anton!" Frau Beisswanger said with a small sigh of exasperation.

For an instant, Anton hesitated. Then, unable to hold

back any longer, he barely nodded his head. His eyes hung on a silver basket on the sideboard, which, in the bustle of the day, must have been left there by the maid since breakfast time.

"One of those little rolls perhaps, if it's no trouble," he said in a low voice, and added anxiously, perhaps interpreting Frau Beisswanger's shocked expression as indignation at his lack of gratitude, "Mother ran out of food for us last night, and I can't eat whipped cream on an empty stomach."

Eva, arriving home with a stomach ache, asked to be excused from supper that evening, and her mother—told about Horst and Anton and the silver basket on the Beisswanger sideboard—shook her head sadly and brewed some peppermint tea for her.

Later, Eva sat in pajamas and robe on the piano bench and watched her father and his friend, Herr Gerber, play a game of chess on the inlaid smoking table between the two arm chairs. The wall clock ticked; Grandfather nodded over his *Thalstadt Guardian*. Her mother sat under the lamp with her needlework, stitching gleaming threads of subtly shaded blues through the stencilled flowers on the linen cloth.

Eva liked watching her father and Herr Gerber play, although the game with its intriguingly carved pieces continued to mystify her. Herr Gerber and her father were old hands at chess, playing together once or twice a month for as long as she could remember. But this evening their faces seemed less intent on their game, as if they were simply going through the accustomed motions, while their minds were on other things. The radio was on, a distraction they would not have allowed themselves in the past; perhaps they were waiting to hear the news when the music stopped. The sound of a horn winged its way lightly, exuberantly, above the strings of the orchestra; a concerto by Mozart, the announcer had said.

When she had gone through her Mozart Sonata with Fräulein Lehmann a few days ago, the piano teacher had told her that she played it "beautifully, but not well." "I can hear how much you love the piece," Fräulein Lehmann had added. "What I can also hear is that you haven't practiced." Eva had promised to do better and started for home, thinking about Arno. Would he be back in the spring? Would he come over, as he had said he would? She could still see him walking next to her with her music sheets under his arm, could feel with the same sharp pang the sudden sideways look he had given her: "What do you think about when you go for walks by yourself?" Mostly about Arno these days, it seemed, though she had never told anyone about him—not Renate, not even Thea.

"Your knight, Gerber," her father was saying.

"*Ja*, Bentheim, there goes my knight—out in the cold, like our former Chancellor, von Papen. Good riddance to him and his cabinet of barons and industrialists—what did he ever do to help the working people!"

"And Hindenburg's new appointee?" Eva's father said. "I hardly consider General von Schleicher an improvement."

"Schleicher . . ." Herr Gerber began, shaking his head and breaking into one of his coughing fits.

Eva, half-listening, felt a chill slither down her back. There was something scary, positively creepy, about a man

whose name meant The Creeper. Evidently Herr Gerber
agreed; for when he stopped coughing, he muttered under
his breath about the Chancellor being "slippery as an eel."

"Schleicher, von Papen—they're two of a kind, Bentheim, intriguing with each other and against each other to
keep old Hindenburg dancing at the end of their strings,"
he went on between moves on the chessboard. "Each thinks
he can use Hitler to advance himself and his clique—play
Cat and Mouse with him. By the time they'll find out who
is the mouse and who is the one with the claws, it'll be too
late. Serves them right, I'd say, except that the real loser
will be the German people."

"It'll start with the Jews," Eva's father said.

"It always does. Labor, the Left, the liberals, the
Jews—they'll be the first to feel the Nazi boot on their
necks. But in the end it will be all of us—Germany, the
world—who'll pay the Pied Piper."

"War?" Eva's father said, moving one of his chessmen.

Herr Gerber shrugged. "If no one stops him here and
abroad, of course Hitler will make war. And get defeated in
the end, I'd be willing to bet. Except . . ."

His broad hand hovered above the chessboard.

". . . except I doubt I'll be around to see the day," he
finished, making his move. "Hold on to your king,
Bentheim. Things don't seem to go very well for either one
of us tonight."

"Herr Gerber, Herr Gerber, you'll be with us for a long
time!" Eva's mother said, putting her needlework down on
her lap. "Why do you make our hearts so heavy? A lot of
water will flow down the Neckar before the Nazis ever take
over in Thalstadt!"

"And you, Eva, why are you up so late? Let the men talk politics into the night if they must—you have school in the morning!"

"Does your stomach still hurt, Eva?" her mother said, coming into her room. She was lying scrunched up under her covers, feeling crampy. Half understood phrases kept tumbling through her head, filling her with apprehension in spite of what her mother had said. Her mother, as usual, knew something was wrong.

She sat down on the edge of the bed. "Would you like the hot-water bottle, Eva?"

"It isn't really my *stomach*," Eva said. "It's right here." She took her mother's hand and put it over the crampy place cradled low between her hips. "Do you think it could be the *Tante aus Amerika?*"

"The *what?*" her mother asked, baffled.

"The Aunt from America—that's what the girls in school call it, Mother, didn't you know? No one in my class has it yet, but some have older sisters who do, so they know all about it. You never told me," she finished reproachfully.

Her mother stroked Eva's cheek with the back of her rough-gentle hand. "I should have. I guess I didn't want to see that my little girl was growing up."

She smoothed Eva's rumpled sheet and quickly kissed her good-night. "Let's talk about it tomorrow, Eva—it's time we do."

8 ❦❦❦

"The times" now had a name. But it was seldom spoken aloud in Eva's house, as if the very word had hidden powers better left uninvoked. "*He,*" she would hear them say over the clatter of coffee cups after dinner, through the cigar smoke in the drawing room next door, "*He* will get in—the Weimar parties are being torn to pieces." "*He?* In an enlightened country like Germany? Ridiculous!" Or: "Have you read *his* book? So have the French—they'll never put up with a loaded pistol pointed at their backs!"

Sometimes, when Eva came into the room, they stopped talking altogether and looked away guiltily, as if they had spoken of something sick or sordid, "not fit for a child's ears."

In the wintry streets, on the walls of buildings and on the newspaper kiosks, the name had a face. A stony face with veiled yet piercing eyes and the incongruous adornment of a trimly cut French general's mustache on the taut upper lip. It was a face no one any longer thought of as that of a funny little man. Now people stopped before the posters on the kiosks and stared at the face and at the thick black slogans beneath it. And out of the corner of her eye, Eve watched them stare and wondered what they were thinking.

When she asked her father, he would shake his head. "Don't ask me to burden you with things you can do nothing about, Eva. Things that may never come to pass, if people wake up before it is too late." He placed his hand on his high forehead in a gesture of infinite weariness. "Enjoy your childhood while you may, Eva. What better place to be a child than Thalstadt. . . ."

Her mother drew her aside. "You mustn't upset your father with those questions, Eva. You know he hasn't been well."

Eva shrugged, impatient with her mother's faulty adult logic. It was "*he*," the face on the kiosk, not she with her questions, who made her father place his hand on his forehead in that unconscious gesture of weariness.

In school, a green and ribboned Advent wreath lay on Frau Ackermann's desk. Each Monday morning she would light one more of the four tall white Advent candles. The schoolroom smelled of pine needles and molten wax.

Frau Ackermann's daily song had given way to Christmas carols.

> *"From Heaven on high I come and sing,*
> *Good tidings to you I shall bring."*

Their voices rang, and the teacher nodded her crisp approval.

"An ancient air, class. Bach's music and the text by Luther himself." She motioned them to their seats.

" 'Good tidings to you I shall bring. . . .' In those days, too, life was bitter in Germany. The peasants were hungry and rose up in bloody revolt against the established order. Luther's Christmas song taught the poor and homeless to put their faith in heaven, in the 'good tidings' from another, better world."

She turned to the window to lower the shade against the glare of the winter sun. In the schoolyard the flower beds were covered with snow, and the gaunt branches of the trees glittered with frost. Frau Ackermann opened the window cautiously and drew a deep breath of the clean, sharp air.

" 'When the need is sorest, God's help is nearest,' " she murmured, almost as if she had forgotten about her class. "Perhaps, once again, a man will rise in Germany to lead us out of the Valley of Darkness."

Behind her back, Horst Reuter's arm shot forward, his outstretched hand pointing toward the blackboard. "Heil Hitler!" he hissed in a loud stage whisper, watching the teacher with narrowed eyes.

Frau Ackermann turned uneasily, as if a wave of discord and hostility had reached her across the candle lights. Her eyes searched the faces of the children bent over their books, rested briefly on Horst's hand lying in limp innocence on his ink-spotted desk. For an instant her lips moved, as if she were about to pose a momentous question, utter a crucial pronouncement. But the moment passed.

"Anton Huber, will you collect the grammar exercises, please!" Frau Ackermann bent over her desk and blew out the Advent candles. One by one the golden flames went out with a faint crackling sound.

Her mother and Anna were in the kitchen, making *Ausstecherle* cookies, when Eva got home from school.

"Ah, Eva, go wash your hands quickly and help Anna

with the baking!" her mother said, untying her apron and handing Eva her own from the nail behind the kitchen door. "Your father has an appointment with Dr. Neuburger, and we were just about to leave."

Eva put down her books. Baking was her favorite helping chore, especially baking cookies with the old-fashioned cutout forms, but today Ella and Uschi were going to the Christmas Fair on the Marktplatz and had asked her to come along.

Her mother was buttoning up her coat. "And when you've finished, Eva, why not run down to the fair for a while? Anna, too, if she'd like."

"I'll treat you to Turkish honey, Anna!" Eva cried.

Anna put down the rolling pin and brushed a speck of flour from her cheek with the back of her hand. Bits of powdered dough clung to her fingers.

"When we've *finished*, Fräulein—you heard your mother!"

Anna took the cookie forms from the cupboard and set them out on the table: stars and rabbits, jagged half-moons, and round-leafed clover.

"You remember from last year, Eva. First you dip the cutters into a little flour, then press down hard into the rolled-out dough."

"Yes, Anna," Eva said, and began to get busy. In the warm kitchen, adding row on row of cookie shapes on the flour-dusted board, the prospect of the fair enticingly ahead, Horst Reuter's hand raised in the Nazi salute seemed very far away.

Later in the street, the fading winter sun suddenly made

her remember the classroom and the teacher's eyes warily searching the faces before her. Even in the milling crowd on the square, Eva felt oddly alone. Without being aware of it, she laid her hand on the fleecy red sleeve of Anna's coat.

Anna gave her a quick look. "What is it, Eva? Didn't things go well in school today? You've been a little too quiet all afternoon."

Eva decided to take the plunge. "It's this Hitler, Anna. Everyone is suddenly talking about him. Worrying about him or saying, 'Heil Hitler!' What's so big about him, anyhow?"

She tried to make it sound as flippant as she could, but she felt Anna's arm stiffen.

"Why?" Anna asked curtly.

"A boy in school . . ." Eva shrugged, suddenly sorry she had begun, suddenly afraid. Perhaps—it was too terrible to contemplate—perhaps Anna *liked* Hitler, or perhaps, as Frau Ackermann had done, she would turn away and talk about something else.

"I don't know a thing about politics, Eva, I've told you before," Anna said, stopping briefly to admire a full-branched Christmas tree on the sidewalk outside the florist's shop. "Where I come from, in our village, girls are not raised to know about such things. But as for Hitler, he is a loud-mouthed good-for-nothing, that much I do know. I'd stay away from anyone who has anything to do with his brownshirts."

She slapped Eva's shoulder and gave it a little shake. "And now enough of this nonsense! Why spoil the fair for ourselves talking about Hitler? He's probably out swilling in some *Bierstube* in Munich!"

She stopped at the first of the wooden booths on the Marktplatz.

"Some Turkish honey for the little *fräulein*, please!" Anna pressed the paper bag of sticky, crunchy sweets into Eva's hand and bought another one for herself. "Nothing like a bit of Turkish honey to put one into a holiday mood, huh, Eva?" she said, popping a big sticky piece of it into her mouth.

They looked at one another, chewing reverently, and burst out laughing.

"We'd better hurry and look around a bit before it gets too dark," Anna said, turning her back on the inviting smile of a well-dressed man in the crowd.

"*Schwarzwaelder Uhren*, Fräulein, Black Forest cuckoo clocks!" a wrinkled, shawled face called out from the next booth.

"*Nuernberger Lebkuchen*," shouted another vendor. "Fine Nuremberg gingerbread!"

The scents of gingerbread, pine needles, and tangerines mingled in the snow-laden air—the scents of Thalstadt at Christmas time, familiar and comforting, even if one's own holiday had a different name.

They walked along the rickety rows of the booths, past the clocks with their carved and painted birds frantically calling time, past the Thuringian glass-blower with his transparent ware of fragile Christmas angels and gnarled Harz Mountain dwarfs.

"Look at the pottery at Herr Marek's stand, Anna!" Eva said, pulling her into a side street.

"Yes, Potter Marek has a good pair of hands," Anna nodded. "Too bad he isn't as fortunate in his daughters."

Her words put a tarnish on the glazed earthenware bowls

and vases that overflowed the pottery shop and lined the sidewalk. The Marek daughters, married and unmarried both, all made their home with the father, selling his wares off the sidewalk and watching a bevy of scantily clad children dash between the cars on the busy street. In the evenings, they took turns walking their father's unkempt sheep dog, Wolf, whose ferocious barking frightened the pigeons off the roof tops and made the neighbors mutter vaguely about summonses and suits. But there was something about the swinging gypsy stride of the Marek daughters, something about their snapping black eyes, and about the shambling figure of the old man, that kept the mutterers from carrying out their threats. Eva had not expected Anna to side with the gossips about his daughters. It was not good to believe too readily what people were saying. Some things, simply by being repeated often enough, had a way of turning out to be true. Or at least, they became *accepted* as being true—which was almost the same thing.

The old man stood bareheaded inside his booth, his shambling figure stooped beneath the low ceiling. His eyes kept a sharp watch on the inquisitive hands of the children in the crowd. One of his daughters, a bright bandana around her raven-black hair, held a brown earthenware vase in her hands, turning it slowly so that the lingering light shone in its richly glazed curves. A young man in a leather jacket, hands in his pockets, stood gazing at the vase, and as her snapping black eyes met his, they seemed to mock him silently, impudently.

"Oh, Anna, there is the patent-medicine man from last year!" Eva tugged at Anna's sleeve until Anna heard her voice above the din of the fairgoers and followed absentmindedly. Eva wondered what Anna had looked at so intently that she had almost forgotten about her.

The crowds around the patent-medicine man were larger than anywhere else at the fair. That was the first thing one noticed. The second was the people at his stand: they were either quite old or else very young. Old men, pinched faces shrunk into upturned collars; old women with limp shopping bags, clutching worn purses and scanning the pillboxes and tonic flasks in the dim interior of the booth. And between them, the children, pressed up close, unmindful of the wind frosting their cheeks, giggling under the acid stare of the medicine hawker, moving on slowly at his querulous biddings to make room for the grown-ups.

Over the shawled heads of the old women and the woolen caps of the children, the hawker's voice rang out shrilly into the sinking dusk.

"Discovered by Dr. Hyroniemus of Leipzig and treated with ultraviolet rays by Professor Dr. Thielemann of Heidelberg. . . ."

He placed a haggard finger on the serpentine maze of glass tubes on the counter. "The human body is a complicated machine, as intricately designed as this patented replica!"

His bony fingers pressed a button and a noxious green fluid spurted up and gurgled through the glass. The children caught their breath and the old people drew closer with a collective murmur of awe.

With practiced hands, the hawker dropped a spoonful of white powder into the glass. The cloudy liquid sputtered and hissed, forming a white crest of foam. When it cleared, after a moment of hushed expectation on the part of the watchers, the liquid was no longer green but a fiery red.

"This is how Dr. Hyroniemus' Life Elixir turns bilious body juices into fresh, rich blood!" the medicine man cried, spreading his hands against the darkening sky. "Life Elixir heals rheumatism, sciatica, neuritis, influenza, anemia, senility. . . ."

His hands flew across the counter, wrapping up pillboxes and tonic bottles, readying change.

The knot of spectators had thinned. The children scattered and a few of the old people walked away, some shrugging their shoulders skeptically, others melting into the crowd with a backward glance of regret. But among those who remained, hands hesitantly reached into pockets and purses, hopefully counting out coins on the grimy counter.

"*Ja*, Granny, now you can throw away that cane and go dancing again," the medicine man said, winking at someone at the edge of the crowd as he took a half-Mark piece from a stooped old woman in exchange for a bottle of tonic. He switched on a bulb that hung forlornly from the roof of the booth. In the hard glare, the liquid inside the bottle was a bilious green. A wave of revulsion seized Eva. The medicine man, who had seemed so amusing the year before, had become subtly transformed, conveying some dark, compelling sense of dread.

"Life   Elixir   heals   sciatica . . . influenza . . . and senility. . . ."

"Potions and promises to make those poor folks hand over their few pennies to you!" A voice rang out from the darkening street.

Heads turned; an old man withdrew his hand and turned his coin over and over in his leathery palm.

The hawker's eyes flickered over the crowd. A young man, hands in his pants pockets, elbowed his way to the stand. Eva recognized the man in the leather jacket whom she had seen at the potter's stand. He turned his back on the medicine man and leaned against the counter, blocking the glass contraption from view.

"God knows it takes more than green water and fancy talk to make our bodies well! It takes jobs and bread and a decent life—and a roof over our heads for our old age. . . ."

There was a wary rumble of voices, an uneasy shuffling of feet.

"The boy's right," said a toothless old man next to Eva. "These glib-talking North German fellows think they can put anything over on us up here."

"I bought a bottle of the stuff last year and it tasted of nothing but brackish water and did no more good than that," said a younger woman in a shabby, ill-fitting coat.

But others looked with hostility at the young man, as if they hated him for destroying their morsel of leftover hope. It was on one of those the medicine man fastened his eyes.

He smiled, a thin, wily smile of confidentiality. "*Ja*, if you'd rather throw your money into the fangs of the *Judendoktors* around here. . . ."

"Nazi!" the young man cried, shaking his fist. "You're one of them all right, claiming to cure our ills by forcing a devil's brew down our throats!"

"Police!" screamed the medicine man. "A troublemaker! An agitator! A communist!" He leaned across the counter, his face livid in the glare of the yellow bulb. "Help! *Polizei!*"

At the cry *police*, the watchers slunk away one by one, as if each of them carried a share of guilt for having listened, for merely having been there when the young man spoke.

An elderly policeman stepped out of the shadows beyond the booth.

"You'd better beat it!" Anna said nervously, tugging at the young man's sleeve.

He gave her a smile that was a little too cocky for the guarded look in his eyes. "Why should I, Fräulein? I've committed no crime."

The medicine man pointed his bony finger at the young man and whispered confidentially into the policeman's ear.

"Your name and occupation?" The policeman pulled out his pad.

"What are you charging me with, officer?" the young man asked quietly.

"Disturbing the peace and interfering with duly licensed commerce!" The policeman wetted the stubby point of his pencil with his tongue.

"But all I've done is tell those poor people to keep their Christmas pfennigs out of that charlatan's hands!"

"He's got a license," the policeman said. "Signed by the bürgermeister of Thalstadt, that's all I know."

"*Ach*, Herr *Wachtmeister*," Anna suddenly spoke up, shrewdly raising the policeman's rank. "Sergeant, this fellow is no agitator. I've known him for years. He is from my village in the Remstal, and he's never harmed a soul in his life!"

Behind the young man's back, she quickly tapped her finger to her forehead and smiled significantly. The policeman tugged at his graying mustaches. "You mean . . .?"

"Yes, Herr *Leutnant*, that's what I mean. *Sie verstehn mich gut!*" Anna said, hugging her red fleece coat snugly over her hips.

For a long moment, the policeman's pencil remained suspended over his pad; then he stuck it into his breast-pocket and shrugged.

"The first thing we'll do is clean out the Weimar Jew-lovers and old women in the police force!" the medicine man shouted, throwing on his coat and fingering the round swastika pin stuck on the narrow lapel.

The policeman drew his stubby finger under the stiff collar of his uniform. "Come along, you!" he commanded curtly, putting his hand on the young man's shoulder. "You're under arrest."

"We'll have to get home, Eva," Anna said. The patent-medicine vendor was shutting down his stand, muttering under his breath and shooting wrathful glances in their direction.

Anna hurried across the square so quickly that Eva could hardly keep pace. She was walking toward the Rathaus, where the little booths were dimming their lights and drawing their shutters. Ahead of them, in the homeward-bound crowd, set apart on a small island of curiosity and awe, were the policeman and his prisoner. Anna, holding firmly to Eva's hand, followed them stubbornly.

Behind the Rathaus, near the entrance to the police station, the policeman suddenly stopped. He glanced about the deserted sidewalk.

"Herr *Wachtmeister!*" Anna cried in a low voice, swiftly coming up behind him. "Remember what I told you!"

The policeman thumped his rubber truncheon against his boots. "I'll let you off this once," he told the young man gruffly. "You've found yourself a good advocate! But learn to hold your tongue. When those gentlemen take over, they won't be so easy on you—nor on the likes of me, either!"

He twirled his rubber truncheon between his stubby fingers and walked away, his helmet gleaming in the light of the street lamp.

"Come on, Eva," Anna said quickly, turning her back on the young man and hurrying up the street. "Your father must be up from the store—it's a good thing I prepared supper in advance."

But Eva would not let Anna change the subject so easily. "Did you really know that young man, Anna? And is he really . . .?" Eva pointed toward her forehead as Anna had.

Anna said nothing. Only her heels clicked on the frosted pavement, almost with an angry sound.

"Not *him*, Eva," she said after a while, "But someone *like* him I did once know, yes. We grew up together, and were to be married; but he was *arbeitslos*, poor and without a job, and he didn't go to church on Sundays. And he talked funny-like, how the meek wouldn't inherit *anything* except if they'd organize and fight for their rights. My father wouldn't let me have him, and he went out into the wide world and I don't know what's become of him; but perhaps someone else will do him a good turn now and then, the way I could help this other one today."

She glanced at Eva with a half-smile. "No, Eva, he *wasn't* what I told the policeman. But, you know, people are quicker to make allowances for those who are queer in the head than for those who are good at heart."

Quick footsteps came up behind them. Even before Eva turned around, she knew whose they were.

He reached into his breast pocket for a rumpled cigarette and lit a match. For a second the flame showed his features in sharp relief—a lean face, not as young as he had seemed at the potter's stand, not as bold as he had appeared when he spoke to the crowd. The leather of his jacket was cracked, and the fingers cupping the flame shook slightly.

He drew a deep puff. "*Danke schön*, Fräulein," he said, shaking Anna's hand.

For a moment they stared at one another, unsmiling, intently.

He is going to kiss her! Eva thought with alarm, for there was in the intentness of their gaze a longing and a sadness, too. At the very least he would take her for coffee and cake at some small *Konditorei* where a wavy-haired pianist coaxed sentimental hit tunes from a rickety upright in the corner. That would be the beginning—and in the end, Anna would leave, as Detta once had.

As if he had guessed Eva's fears, the young man dropped his hand and lowered his eyes from Anna's, breaking the spell.

"I am out of work," he said softly, as if in answer to an unspoken question. A moment later he was gone, swallowed up in a patch of darkness between the streetlights.

9 ❦❦❦

December turned into January. In the park the frozen pond glittered within the circling hedge of its barren shrubs; and where in summer the swans would glide silently across the water, now the swish of skates and the skaters voices filled the clear air. Strains of the "Skaters' Waltz" blared from the wooden shed where hot cocoa and sugar wafers were sold. Ella and Eva joined the line inside, wobbling stiffly on their skates over the mud-streaked planks.

"Hurry, slowpoke!" Ella called back, having shouldered her way to the counter with her customary efficiency. She balanced her steaming cup in her mittened hand and tore the cellophane wrapper off her wafer with her front teeth. "Come on, Eva, if you want to skate some more before dark!"

But when Eva finally had her turn at the counter, she found that she had left her change purse with her school things at home. Visions of the small red pouch, wedged between the hard cover of her nature study book and the soft, dog-eared one of her Uhland ballads, hovered vexingly in the noise-filled air. She felt in her ski-pants pockets for a stray ten-pfennig piece, but there was none.

Ella, it turned out quickly, had used up her allowance on modeling clay; she was currently on an elephant binge, and Uncle Ludwig would show off her droopy-eared creatures with a deprecating shrug that fooled no one. After a visible struggle, Ella held her cocoa cup under Eva's nose. "Not that you *deserve* it, Eva—always misplacing and forgetting things. If your head wasn't fastened on to your neck . . ."

Eva glared at her cousin, torn between her dignity and the chocolaty vapors rising irresistibly from Ella's cup. Just as she had shamelessly settled for the latter and bent her head toward that first, tongue-scalding sip, Ella hastily snatched back her hand.

"Hold it, Eva! You'd better think this over! I mean with Uschi having the measles, I wouldn't want you to catch any germs from my cup."

Eva could have wept with disappointment. With measles at the Upstairs, her mother had been reluctant to let her go skating with Ella, let alone having her drink from an Upstairs' cup! There was nothing left to do but watch her cousin drink up and toss the drained and crumpled paper cup on an overflowing trash can.

"Well, are you coming, Eva?" Ella asked and stalked toward the door.

Shivering with cold and self-pity, Eva leaned her elbow against the counter and shifted her feet to ease the pressure of the skates against her soles.

"Hey, Eva Bentheim, don't take up space at the counter if you're not buying cocoa!" a high-pitched boy's voice sang out behind her. It was Anton Huber, carefully filling rows of paper cups from a round-bellied pitcher that seemed too heavy for his skinny arms.

"I'm helping Frau Hauff," he explained, and hastily

wiped up a trickle of spilled liquid with a large towel already none too clean. "Sundays and after school. Mother can use the extra money, and"—he grinned the wry smile that crinkled his eyes now and then—"I can have all the hot cocoa I want."

"But your homework, Anton. When do you find time for that?"

It seemed wrong for Anton to spend his free hours working when Eva knew very well how worried he was about keeping up his grades.

Anton shrugged and pushed back a strand of his sandy hair with the crook of his arm. "Oh, I manage. My father is still out of work, and he's very good at arithmetic. I'm sorry, Eva, you'll really have to move on. Frau Hauff gives me a scolding when I hold up the line talking to kids from school."

But just as she turned to leave, Anton caught the fringe of her scarf. He scanned her face shrewdly. "You've no money, Eva. That's it, isn't it?"

"I left my change purse at home," Eva mumbled.

Anton tucked the towel under his arm and fished a ten-pfennig piece from his pocket. "Take it, Eva. I'll get my day's pay when I'm through tonight, and you can pay me back in school tomorrow."

"First thing in the morning!" She suddenly realized that she was not only tired and cold but also hungry; her stomach felt queasy and her head swam. "Could you possibly spare another tenner, Anton?" she heard herself ask to her own great surprise, tearing her eyes from the tray full of wafers Frau Hauff was bringing from the other end of the counter. "Just till tomorrow, I promise."

"It's in their *blood*, it's *always* been in their blood!" A tight voice spoke up at her back. Frau Hauff had come up behind her, the tray with the wafers pressed against her cocoa-spattered apron. "Borrowing and lending, charging interest and getting rich on our hard work. Don't you go around loaning your tenners to the likes of *her*, boy—not as long as it's tenners you get from *me*. It's *her* kind that put your father on the breadlines and ruined the land with their usury and greed!"

Somewhere, just on the other side of the counter and yet miles away in a drift of chocolate-flavored mist, Anton stood staring at Eva, his hand, with the coin between his fingers, suspended in the air as if it were no longer a part of him. A freckle-faced boy in the line laughed overly loud and whispered something to a girl in a white felt skirt. The other children looked away, their faces closed-off, blank. Eva wanted to run; but her feet felt strangely weighted, as if her skates had dug deep grooves into the wooden plank, pulling her down and down.

"Go on, you, don't hold up those having an honest piece of change!" Frau Hauff shouted, her eyes moist with loathing behind her thick, fogged lenses.

Her hand clamped over Anton's like a vise. A spasm of pain rent his thin face, and the coin dropped from his stiffened fingers and clattered along the counter.

Eva turned and hobbled awkwardly through the receding crowd of staring faces. For a moment she thought she heard Anton call her name, and in the instant before she glanced back, she imagined him calmly pocketing his coin and throwing the soiled towel into Frau Hauff's astonished face. But the coin was still on the counter, glistening innocently in the light overhead, and Anton, bent over the round-bellied pitcher, was filling two paper cups for the freckle-faced boy and the girl in the white felt skirt.

Outside, bright scarves flew in the gathering dusk; skates skimmed the glittering mirror of ice under the floodlights. The strains of the "Skaters' Waltz" filled the air, and at the edge of the park, the white pillars of the Staatstheater gleamed through the evergreens.

She said nothing to Ella, who was in a benevolent mood on the way home (a boy she knew had pitched a snowball at her and she, declining the compliment, had sent him skidding to the ground with a well-aimed fusillade of her own). They walked home slowly under the bare-branched trees, across the lawn where once, long ago, Ella had explained to her the facts of life. It happened on an Easter Sunday morning, Eva recalled. A girl wearing a straw hat with yellow daisies and a velvet streamer down her back had asked Eva "what she was," *katholisch* or *evangelisch?* While Eva stood in confusion, trying to decide between the two unfamiliar words, Ella had ordered her to tell the girl that she was *juedisch*—and that she was never to forget it again. And when she wondered why Ella was so angry, and why the girl in the daisy hat looked at them curiously and suddenly turned on her black patent-leather heels and skipped across the lawn as if she had shrugged some burdensome weight off her shoulders, Ella had unaccountably bent down to her, straightened the bow of her middy blouse, and explained that Catholic and Lutheran children went to church on their holidays and Jews went to synagogue on theirs; and that there was nothing to be ashamed about being different—only about not wanting to tell it.

"You didn't *know*," Ella added, unaccustomedly gentle, seeing Eva's eyes fill with confusion and remorse. "You didn't know—you're too little."

It seemed odd, now, that there had ever been a time when Eva had not known she was *juedisch*—and what it *meant* to be Jewish. It meant Frau Hauff saying "the likes of *her*," and Anton hiding his eyes behind the pitcher; it meant the children in the shed drawing back to form an almost palpable wall between them and her. She glanced at Ella: her heavy brows were knotted in their habitual scowl, but her face was softened with a secret smile; her dark hair peeked from under the red woolen cap, and her hand holding the strap of her skates (she had lost one of her mittens in the victorious snowball skirmish with her admirer) was chapped from the wind as anyone's hand would be. There seemed no reason why she should be loathsome or hateful to *anyone*; but when Frau Hauff had said "it's in their blood," she had meant Ella too.

Eva remembered, suddenly, the time she had fallen at the Upstairs' and gashed her head, dark rivulets of blood matting her hair. "Eva is *dying!*" Uschi had screamed; and Emma, Aunt Gustl's cook, had rushed into the room and stayed the red flow with her handkerchief. "Hush, Uschi," Emma had said, "it's nothing to be afraid of—just a wee bit of blood, same as yours or mine."

But that had been long ago, before the speeches and the posters and the singing, shouting marchers in the streets. . . .

"Look, Eva," Ella was saying, her voice entering Eva's thoughts from far away. "You've been sulking long enough.

It wasn't *my* fault you left your change purse at home."

She held out a handful of burnt almonds. Ella had a passion for burnt almonds and usually hoarded a few in her pockets, where they became damp and sticky and coated with bits of lint. Eva took some to prove she was not sulking. But when Ella was not looking, she dropped them one by one to the cobblestones of the Schillerplatz. Her mouth felt dry; it seemed suddenly a great effort to put one foot in front of the other, as if each step had to be planned carefully in one's head. Or perhaps it was that her head was so busy thinking about other things: the questions she would put to her father this evening, no matter *what* her mother would say. She would not be put off any longer about Hitler and the terrible things he was saying and people were beginning to believe—or had perhaps *always* believed, merely waiting for someone to say them out loud. She had to *know*—all of it—even if the things they were saying turned out to be true.

10 ⅄⅄⅄

Anna was singing softly in the kitchen:

> *"There fell a frost in a night of spring,*
> *It fell on the tender young flowers blue,*
> *They withered away and wilted . . ."*

Curled up on top of her bed, Eva was looking over the long division that Fräulein Kessler, the math teacher, had assigned. But her eyes hurt; it was better to close them and listen to Anna.

> *"There was a boy who loved a girl,*
> *They ran in secret away from home,*
> *And told neither father nor mother . . ."*

She had heard Anna sing this song many times before, and always the words had painted a picture for her: a flowery meadow under a dark spring sky, and a boy and girl running over the meadow with their arms about each other. They never came close enough so she could see their faces. But the girl with the braids down her back would be Anna. She was running away with her childhood sweetheart, the one her father would not let her marry because he was poor and out of work.

> *"They wandered together here and there,*
> *Had nor good fortune nor lucky star,*
> *They wasted away and perished."*

Eva turned around with a start.

"It's the likes of *you* put him on the breadlines," a bitter voice was whispering in the empty room. Her feet felt like ice in their warm felt slippers. The figures in her book flared and dissolved.

Her mother was calling to her from the door. Eva had not heard her come in; now her face looked blurred against the stab of light from the hallway.

"Grandfather and I are going to Aunt Hanni's for a while, Eva. Don't stay up late—you looked rather peaked at supper."

As soon as Eva heard the front door close behind them, she shut her book and went into the living room.

Her father sat in his chair by the window, the unread evening paper folded on his knees. He had taken off his glasses and was polishing the lenses with his handkerchief; Eva could see the deep, bruised ridge the metal frame left on the bridge of his nose. As always without the glasses, his eyes looked vulnerable, exposed.

He stirred uneasily and looked up. "Coming to keep me company, Eva? Sit down and talk to me for a while."

She sat down stiffly on the black piano bench, avoiding his eyes. Her heart hammered against her chest, which felt queerly tight and ached with each breath. When she spoke, her voice sounded thin and whiny, but she knew she had to say it quickly or she would never say it at all.

"Is it true that we put Anton's father on the breadlines?"

There—it was out and she was glad of it, through suddenly afraid, too, now that the words hung between them in the quiet room, never to be retrieved.

Her father fumbled with his glasses and finally returned them to their accustomed place, hiding the deep reddened ridge. Behind the glasses, his eyes rested on Eva with an expression of ancient pity.

It was not what she had expected to find. Shock, yes; indignation, yes: for these she had hoped. Or anger: for if there were guilt, there would be anger. But pity? She could neither cope with it nor understand it.

"That is perhaps the hardest thing to bear," she heard her father say softly after a long while, during which there had been only the ticking of the old wall clock, unhurried, imperturbed. "To see a child's trust destroyed, to have to vindicate one's life to one's own child. . . ."

He got up heavily and leaned his forehead against the window. Across the street, the tall, stark structure of Hallenbeck's store loomed darkly in the night. From somewhere in the city came the distant roll of drums, the thud of marching boots.

She slipped her hand in her father's and felt his fingers close about her own. How firm and warm his grip was; only once before had he held her like this. They had gone for a boat ride on one of the sputtering little motorboats with bright pennants that dot the Neckar in the summertime. She had been afraid to step off the dock into the shaky boat until her father's hand had steadied her, making her brave. Perhaps this, too, was the beginning of a journey. She wondered where it would lead.

"No, Eva," her father was saying. "You need not carry the burden of guilt along with the pain of persecution. The things you heard said—and will hear again and again—these things are not true."

Her throat was burning. "Then why do they *say* them? Why do they *believe* them?"

Her father shook his head. "There are many answers, Eva: facile answers, learned answers, angry answers. Some say that we are made to suffer for our sins—though our lives seem no more sinful to me than those of *any* human beings: a little less so, perhaps, because the greatest sin is to deny the humanness of another—and God, by keeping us powerless, has in His wisdom by and large reserved that sin for others."

"Is it because of Jesus?" she persisted.

"That fierce and gentle Hebrew rebel," her father said sadly, "would rage and weep over the age-old carnage of his flesh."

"*When Jewish blood . . . spurts from our knives . . .*" the marchers sang below, swinging into the square around the corner of Grandfather's house. They disappeared into the darkness beyond St. Christopher's Church, where Anna knelt on Sundays beneath the suffering Christ, his body pierced by other soldiers' blades.

What was it her father was saying?

". . . my good friend Gerber, a Christian who follows his own Jewish savior, Marx, tells me it is 'the System.' The rich and powerful, he says, use us for scapegoats—make people blame 'the Jews' instead of the industrialists who exploit them, the generals who kill off their sons in wars, the bankers who foreclose their farms, the governments who do the bidding of the bankers, the generals, the industrialists. . . ."

He shrugged. "Perhaps. But what if *his* System will need scapegoats too? It seems not so much a matter of the *kind* of system but of its *quality*. The less perfect a society is, the less it permits its people to dream, to act, to question, to protest—the more it needs its Jews to hide behind, even if it has to invent them."

Her head reeled. "Diete Goetz says the Jews run the country. Horst Reuter says the Jews made Germany lose the war."

Her father nodded. "We are the river into which men cast their guilt and shame. Their secret fears, their drives, their emptinesses, their uncertainties. Each age, each place, creates the Jew in its own image; that is why none of the answers tell the full story. Only history may tell, someday —a long time off, I suppose."

"When the Messiah comes?" Eva asked, half wanting to believe the ancient story, half knowing that her father would smile at her childish question.

"Yes, Eva, in the time of the Messiah: the time of that kinder, wiser, truly *human* being who may yet evolve from what mankind is today—if the world can keep itself running long enough."

He put his arm about her shoulder. "Can you try to live so as to help bring that time a little bit closer, Eva? And believe in yourself—in who you are and what you are—no matter what lies ahead?"

It seemed a great deal to ask of a mere schoolgirl. Holding on to her father's hand, the ground swaying beneath her feet like the time she had stepped into the river boat, Eva barely managed to nod her head.

Anna came into the room to put a pan of apples into the green-tiled oven. "Herr Bentheim, you oughtn't keep Eva up this late," she said reproachfully. "And with that draft from the window! The child has a fever; take a look at her eyes. She must've caught the measles from the Upstairs."

It was enough to make Eva giggle. "I *can't* have the measles, Anna!" she sputtered, surprised to hear her teeth chatter when she felt so warm. "I didn't drink from Ella's cup. And Anton wanted to loan me ten pfennig for cocoa, but Frau Hauff wouldn't let him, because . . ."

It hurt her chest to go on, but it would have hurt even more to stop.

Her father was bending over her, his eyes anxious. "We won't talk about it now, Eva. Let Anna help you to bed. But I will speak to Frau Hauff tomorrow; it is not yet too late. She has no right to hurt and humiliate a child. . . ."

But it *was* the measles. And it *was* too late.

It snowed that night, and the next morning rose with a white and brilliant sun. Later, Dr. Neuburger came, with his shuffling walk and his soggy cigar, and ordered the blinds drawn to shield her eyes against the glittering brightness outside. Eva heard him speak to her mother in the hallway; and when she came back, carrying a cool, raspberry-tinted drink on a little round tray, she smiled at Eva with lips suddenly gone white. Eva was much too sick to ask questions. The house was mute; even the radio remained shut off—so the music wouldn't hurt her head, they said.

It was only later, when Eva was allowed to sit up in bed again and, resting listlessly against the pillow propped at her back, begged for the radio to be turned on, that she found out.

On that day of snowy glitter and sparkling skies, Hitler had been appointed Chancellor of Germany.

A dream came back to her then, from one of the nights of her raging fever. She was on the Schlossplatz with Uschi; they sat on the pavilion steps, listening to the band concert and sifting into their white-pleated skirts the white and fragile chestnut blossoms that drifted from the tall trees like a fine swirl of snow.

Then the music stopped; a hush sank over the square, and when her eyes sought the Marble Column glinting in the sunlight, the Angel of Peace had vanished from its crown. The leaves whispered *"the golden angel vanished . . ."* and gazing down on her lap, she saw that the petals were blighted and tinged with the color of blood. And the leaves and the grass and the houses beyond the square and the hills beyond the city—all, all were steeped in the fallen blossoms: a crimson snow.

EDITH BAER was born in Germany and came to this country in 1940 in her mid-teens, the only member of her immediate family to survive the Holocaust. She worked at a variety of jobs, attending high school and college at night. After marrying and raising a daughter and son, she returned to college to earn a bachelor's degree in English literature, and then a master's degree in library services from Rutgers University. She has written for national magazines and is the author of two books for young children, *The Wonder of Hands* and *Words Are Like Faces!* (Pantheon). *A Frost in the Night* is Edith Baer's first novel. She is now writing a sequel which follows the Bentheim family into the Hitler years. She and her husband live in New Jersey.